COLDEST WINTER

Credits:

Once again may I thank my editor and proof reader, Michael Glanister for finding the typos and faults that I missed.

And typesetter Jo Smith for putting the script in order for the printer.

And of course my friends in East Hampshire Writers who have had to listen and comment on my readings from this text. Thank you all.

Author's note:

My previous novels have taken place in summer with warm seas and sailing boats.

I have set this novel as a contrast in an imaginary coldest winter for one hundred years.

I only hope it does not come across as too Scandinavian and dismal. In contrast part of this story is set in New Zealand in the hottest January for many years. Previous characters Tom and Emily and Emily's parents Steve and Kirsten take part, but I am kinder to them in this book. Their friend Dave Manning the New Zealander takes a central part instead; and meets a frightening climactic moment and final revelation.

Cover design by Peta Print

COLDEST WINTER

James Morley

Coldest Winter
First published 2015

Published by Benhams Sea Mysteries, 1 Fir Cottage, Greatham, Liss, Hampshire GU33 6BB
Typeset by John Owen Smith

ISBN 978-0-9548880-9-1

Printed by CreateSpace

PROLOGUE

The mini-bus was dirty and had two dents on its side. It was three a.m. when it left the Bristol road and turned into the precinct in front of the jail. The vehicle had no lights showing and the driver cut the engine as he carefully parked clear of the floodlights, out of sight of the CCTV camera and near a side door. The driver peered into the passenger area at the back and then descended to the concrete outside. He strode with an air of confidence to the side door and typed in a key code on the security pad. The door opened and he greeted another figure on the inside. 'I've got 'em,' he said. 'All out cold and sleeping.'

'Can they walk?' the new figure sounded nervous.

'Yes, they'll walk if I tell them. They don't like me.'

Four small shadowy figures dismounted from the mini-bus and shuffled sleepily to the open door.

'Put'em in the cellar and I'll be back same time tomorrow.' He paused. 'What about my money?'

'Don't worry, Mr Jones. We used the office phone when the screws weren't around. The dosh is in your bank account safe and sound.'

The door was shut and the mini-bus drove away.

CHAPTER 1

'That vicar's a woman,' Tom frowned.

'Well, why not?' Emily replied. 'Lots of them are now. I keep telling you to join the real world.'

They were standing outside the little Anglican church on the Auckland waterfront. Surrounding them were the wedding guests waiting to enter for the service.

'Well, you believe all this religious stuff,' Tom replied.

'All right, we were married in church and you were fine with that.'

Emily was not going to allow her husband's misogynist grumbling to spoil the day. Here they were, in the hot December sunshine of New Zealand to witness the wedding of their special friends, Josie and David. Neither Emily nor Tom could ever forget that terrible day when their little baby, Peter, had been snatched by a mad psychopath. Now Peter was there by her side in his little push chair. His gurgling speech was just starting to make sense, while lately his floor crawling was beginning to change to a few unsteady upright steps.

Emily was rather pleased to find that New Zealanders followed the same wedding rituals as were practiced in the UK. The TV and news cameras were assembling. Emily guessed these people were less interested in the happy pair than in the matron of honour. Chloe, the local sporting heroine was their Olympic gold medal winner. She, with Emily and their friend Erin had been the three girl match racing crew who had taken gold in the sailing Olympics in the South American republic of Olifa. Chloe, the ebullient New Zealand Maori was also an officer in the British army and as such had qualified to race for Great Britain.

'Come on,' said Tom. 'They're all going inside.'

'Yes,' said Emily. 'And stop ogling that bridesmaid.'

'All right, but she'd never get away with a dress that low cut in an English wedding.'

Even Tom had to admit the church service was a delight. The woman vicar presided over the ceremony and the bride and groom took their oaths without faltering. The singing from the Maori choir was stunning. Then they were outside in the hot sunshine and taking their transport for the short run to the reception in the yacht club. This yacht club might have a royal appellation but it was a typical Kiwi place: laidback, with panoramic views of both of Auckland's harbours. Yes, certainly the girls were suntanned and beautiful, the champagne was the real thing and the wedding breakfast was of gourmet standard. All this, apart from the girls, had been donated by the couple's Australian friend, Donna Crickerman. That extrovert lady was already over there in deep conversation with Chloe and Josie's mother and step-father. It was Donna who had set David on his way to exposing the Hamble murderer. This was an occasion with a chance to mix with old friends from the world of sailing. Tom remembered that Emily and Chloe had been to Auckland for an Olympic indicator meeting five years ago. It was here that they had first encountered today's bridegroom, Dave Manning. Dave, the Kiwi yachting journalist had not been Emily's favourite person that time when he reported her clash with the girl's hated rivals. Everything had changed when Dave came to work in London and played a major part in catching the mad person who had threatened them. Now there was Emily chatting happily with the same three hated rivals of long ago, but now friends.

Emily looked up to see the bridegroom Dave, champagne glass in hand grinning at her. 'Hi there you guys. Great day, great people, eh?'

'Oh, Dave, it was a wonderful ceremony.' Emily raised her own glass. 'We all wish both of you a long and happy life.'

'Tom tells me married life suits him,' Dave laughed. 'By the way,' he dropped his voice. 'Don't tell the vicar, but Josie's expecting – she's three months in.'

'Oh, Dave, that's great. You'll be a complete family, just like us.'

'Thanks, Em. I'd better go, my lady is calling.' Emily could see Josie smiling at her man. She really looked stunning in her white off-shoulder wedding gown.

'Hi you three, how's it going?' Emily was happy to see these friends again, hated rivals no more. Sammy, Tanya and Tracie had fought Emily, Chloe and Erin boat for boat in a thrilling race in the harbour right here in Auckland. Chloe and crew had won but very narrowly and then suddenly the silly feud had melted away. Motherhood and marriage had broken up Sammy's crew and it was Chloe and their crew who had won the Olympic selection but only after three more years of competition and fitness training that Emily would rather forget.

'Em,' said Sammy. 'Is it true you're prosecuting that horrible little perv?'

Emily was dragged back into her real world. As a rising young barrister she had her first high-profile case to put before a court.

'Get him sent to the nick long term,' Sammy glowered.

'Well, the evidence is pretty damning but I guess he'll be fined and put on the sex-offenders list.'

The tabloids had been full of eighty-six-year-old Ferdinand Lord Modlington. Ferdy was a one time politician and cabinet minister who had been found to be in possession of a stack of pornographic CDs entitled: *Sex and the Single School Girl*. Emily's mentor, Tony Travis QC, had handed this high-profile job to her. Travis was prosecuting a much murkier child murderer and in six months time that would be the case the tabloids would slobber over. Right now she would rather forget all this and enjoy the happy day. Anyway the sun was shining, now was summer down under, and tomorrow they would all be going sailing. Emily had no wish to reconnect with the competitive scene. She would never go back to those years of obsession, tunnel vision and the fitness regime that one needed for Olympic qualification. Tom had bought a little sailing cruiser and was basing her in the marina at Hamble, but not the marina where the murder had taken place. Next summer they could sail the Solent and maybe along the coast to Tom's parents in Dorset. In a few year's time they would buy a little Oppie dinghy for Peter to sail. Yes, poor Peter. She knew what he needed was a sibling a brother or sister. Well, back home again, whether Tom liked the idea or not, he would do his family duty.

CHAPTER 2

Twenty-four hours in flight was not something either Emily or Tom had enjoyed. Dave and Josie were staying on in New Zealand for a month. They would tour the land visiting relatives, enjoy the sunshine and do plenty of sailing. Then they would also be back in the UK where Dave would resume his journalism and Josie would complete her latest romantic novel. On arrival Tom was relieved to find his car in the Heathrow car pound was unharmed and ready to take the three of them home to Hampshire. At three o'clock in the afternoon they reached their little family home on the edge of woods and fields in the village of Bishop's Sutton. Emily still loved it despite its associations with that terrifying day when little Peter had been snatched.

'Sleep tonight and back to work tomorrow,' Tom sighed.

'I don't have to work until Thursday,' Emily replied. 'But I'm taking Peter over to see Mum and Dad tomorrow. And I've got the wedding video to show them.'

'They've got our new boat in the yard,' said Tom. 'Let's go see her on the weekend and have a meal out. Why not take Peter and Lily with us?'

'I'm not sure that Lily goes much on sailing but she'll enjoy the meal.' Lily was now part of the family. She was the village lady who came in daily to clean and tidy the house when Tom and Emily were away at work. A mother of older children, Lily had bonded with Peter and in that climactic moment with the mad person she had been stabbed defending the child and taken to hospital. The wound had turned out to be superficial but the fact of it had made her their close friend for life.

'What do we do now?' Emily yawned.

'I think I want to sleep and sleep,' Tom replied. 'Tomorrow is another day.'

The driver swung the steering wheel as he powered the prison van out into the main street by the jail. He was by now used to the stares of passers-by and their rude gestures. He loved driving big wagons, although personally he would rather be operating one with a more desirable cargo in the rear. This time he only had three passengers: two prison officers and a suspect on his way to a prison in central

London nearer to the law courts.

Well, would he tell his grandchildren that he once drove this notorious mass murderer?

By that time the case would no longer scream from the tabloid headlines of the Daily Banner and all the others. An hour later he left the motorway onto a single carriageway A-road. This early in the morning there was little or no traffic around which suited him. Now he sighed in exasperation as there ahead was a police car and a cross-road barrier.

'Very sorry, but there's been an incident,' said the copper. 'Would you please reroute down there.' The man pointed to a turning on the left that the driver knew intersected with that lonely winding road that led into the Sussex Downs. Well, there was nothing for it, the diversion would add half an hour onto this journey; he would just have to live with it. He signalled left, not that there was anyone in the rear and drove on. Three miles further he rounded a bend and then slammed on the brakes. Ahead of him, across the road was a massive farm tractor and trailer. It was stuck, seemingly non-moving, and there was no driver in the cab. Oh, God, it was developing into one of those days.

What happened next was swift and bewildering. A white van had closed up behind and from it sprang four men. They wore hoods and full face masks and were dressed all in black. Now he heard the crash of a metal bar forcing the rear door. He heard the shouts and yells and then he saw it happen. Two black-clad figures were dragging the prisoner towards an oak tree by the roadside and from a branch was suspended a rope with a noose. Two more of these intruders were standing with the prison officers and each pointing at them a handgun. The driver could no longer look. He crouched down on his seat and covered his eyes. After a few minutes he looked up. The body dangled lifeless from the tree. Now there came more real horror. The two prison officers were being forced to kneel. Then a bulky black-clad man shot them, both of them in the back of the head. The driver in desperation remembered his childhood as he made the sign of the cross. But they didn't come for him. The men piled back into the white van that reversed away tyres screaming. The driver was left alone amidst this scene of carnage. Somehow he was able to fumble in his pocket and pull out his mobile phone. And of course, stranded here in the shadow of the hills, there was no signal.

Tom had left for work at eight o'clock the next morning. Emily was due to visit her parents' home in Sussex with Peter and her account and video of the Auckland wedding. And now of course there was a power cut. So nothing would work. She wanted to boil a kettle and sit by the TV and take in the news and local chat. She rummaged in a cupboard and pulled out a battered whistling kettle, rinsed it and made her morning coffee. Without power the central heating had cooled and Emily was anxious for Peter. The sooner she had him in a warm car and away the better. Well, her ancestors had coped without electricity or gas and without motor cars for that matter. In the remote countryside there had been rumours about metal thieves taking electric cable for scrap. How they did this without electrocuting themselves was a mystery.

With Peter safely in his baby seat Emily drove her car the twenty-five miles to her parents' home. Firs Farm the old Georgian farmhouse in Sussex had been her childhood home. It was in the nearby village of South Marshall that she had known Richard Pembelty, the old Air Force veteran who had saved her life all those years ago. And it seemed long ago now and, thank goodness, since Peter was born her nightmares had almost ceased. She had passed the town of Petersfield and reached the village when, to her irritation, she found the road from there onwards was closed. Barriers lay across its width guarded by police. 'Sorry, Madam,' said a formidable looking copper, 'but the road is closed through a serious incident. May we redirect you?'

'But I'm only going to my mum and dad's house and it's just round the corner.'

'If you would give me the name and address of the occupants please?'

Emily gave the man a plaintive glance. 'They're Sir Stephen and Lady Simpson and they live at Firs Farm.'

'And you are?'

Emily rummaged in her handbag and found her driving licence and her courtroom ID. 'I'm Emily Stoneman, but that's my married surname.'

The policeman radioed someone and she was told she could proceed but only as far as the house. Well, what the hell was happening? This looked a bit more serious than a road accident.

It seemed as if half the Sussex constabulary were deployed just along this stretch of road. She reached the entrance of Firs Farm and yet another policeman held up an imperious hand and directed her into the driveway where she wanted to go anyway.

She released Peter, bundled him up and almost ran indoors. 'Mum,

11

Dad what's happening?'

Her mother appeared and she looked grim. 'Haven't you heard? It's all over the news and the television.'

'I haven't heard any news. We've a bloody great power failure at home and I haven't seen any telly.'

'There's been a mass killing only a few miles south of here.' Kirsten, her mother filled her in with the details as far as anyone knew them. 'They haven't named the prison officers yet, but the man lynched is Jebbs the mass murderer.'

'There's plenty of people will say that's justice,' said Steve, Emily's father, who had just come into the room.

'He's due in court and Tony Travis is prosecuting,' said Emily. 'But for God's sake it can't be justice until he's been tried by a court and sentenced.'

'Well it's too late now. Are you saying he might not have done it?'

Emily shook her head. 'No, Tony told me the evidence was conclusive including the forensic reports. It's just that these things should be settled by a jury. For God's sake this is England not the wild west.'

'It's coming up to one o'clock,' said her mother. 'Let's see if there's anything more on the news.'

They all crowded into the sitting room with its wide TV picture screen on the wall.

The television reporter was standing in the nearby village street by the pub.

'We now have some more details. It is confirmed that the murdered prisoner was Arthur Jebbs and police have now released the names of the two murdered prison officers. We understand that their families have been informed. They have been named as: Samuel Jones and Wallace Markham...

'Oh, no,' Emily gasped.

'What's wrong?' asked her mother.

'It's Wally, we know him and he is a prison officer, we know his wife Lorraine and their kids. They sail at Hamble. Lorri was my midwife.'

Kirsten put her arms round her daughter. 'Oh Emily I'm so sorry. It can be a horrible small world sometimes.'

'I'll have to call Josie and Dave in New Zealand. Wally and Lorraine were their friends. They used to race RS 200s together. They were close.' Now she sobbed as she clung to her mother. 'Oh God,

12

even if Jebbs was no loss why did they have to kill Wally and the other man. They were only doing their jobs.'

Chief Constable Norman Fox O.B.E. could have done without this furore. He was only six months away from a well-earned retirement and now he was at the centre of a nationwide sensation. He had called a meeting of his senior CID officers for twelve that morning and following that he would have to hold an après conference briefing and see off a hysterics of press and paparazzi. His officers would do their duty and far more to solve this triple murder, but he wished he did not detect an undercurrent. Jebbs was wholly evil, they could all agree about that, but a lynching was a heinous crime and must never be allowed to become a precedent. There was also this stupid prejudice against prison staff: at least one of his colleagues had muttered about "those two screws". The worst aspect had been in the prison van driver's statement. He had been rerouted by fake policemen with a fake police car. The trouble was that authentic looking police vehicles were available for film and TV work and likewise authentic police uniforms.

He stared once more at the large scale ordnance map. The murders had been on a quiet back road that he knew well, in fact it had been in a bend of the road three miles from South Marshall where his old friends the Simpson family lived. His own wife had worked for Steve Simpson's sail making company in her younger days before their children were born. As a very junior officer he had been involved in the unmasking of the criminal blackmailer, Lindgrun, who had threatened the Simpson family.

The internal phone was ringing and he picked up the receiver. 'Sir, we've traced the tractor and trailer. It was stolen from a farm about five miles away from the crime scene.' The speaker gave details: the farm's address and location.

'Any evidence?' asked Fox.

'Sir, I understand forensics are working on the tractor and the farm now but no positive reports so far.'

Fox was still waiting for a report from the prison service. He wanted a list of former inmates who might have a particular grievance against the two prison officers. Those two inoffensive men had been coldly executed whereas the van driver had been ignored. Very possibly the gang had left the latter unharmed so that he could tell the world. Another sign of this gang's declaring their self-confidence or arrogance. Well, in Fox's experience such arrogance could lead to discovery. He recalled the so called Great Train Robbery.

There came a knock on his office door. Yes, here were his officers for the strategy meeting.

Dave Manning had to admit it. He was serenely happy. He was now committed; married to his wonderful English girl. Josie and he had been together for four years and that was enough for them to discover each other's faults and foibles. He adored Josie and she was expecting their first child. Life would never be better and here they were in the summer sunshine of New Zealand, not the winter gloom back home. Inwardly he groaned; he was doing it again – thinking of England as home. No, he was a Kiwi and this lovely land was his home. The UK was where he had a career and it was Josie's homeland and always would be. He could see Josie sunning herself on the beach near their hired sailing dinghy pulled up above the tideline. His mobile was ringing for the third time that day. The first callers had been the London office of The Daily Banner. Well, yes he worked freelance for the Banner as a sports reporter, even though he had pleased the crime editor with his investigation earlier that year. But he resented them mucking up his honeymoon and why call him at a time that must be around midnight in the UK? He checked the screen of his phone. Yes, this call came from the UK but it was morning there now and the call was from their friend Emily. This time he would answer, and all of a sudden he felt this creeping apprehension.

Josie had just rolled languidly onto her back when she saw her new husband sprinting across the sand to her. She sat up and stared. There was something about his face that was wrong. 'Oh, sweetheart, I just don't know how to tell you this,' Dave looked anguished.

'It's all right, darling. If something's wrong then spit it out.'

Dave seemed anxious. 'I don't want to upset you, not with the baby inside you.'

Josie grinned. 'Stop all that down-under macho male stuff and just tell me.'

'Emily Stoneman's just phoned from England. Something terrible's happened.' Then he told her.

Josie was stunned. Lorraine was her friend and she played with Lorraine's children. Lorraine rarely talked about her husband's work, except that it was a steady job with reasonable pay and it could at times be stressful. Wallace and Lorraine sailed at Hamble on the weekends and she and Dave raced against them in dinghy events on that water.

'Oh God, how awful. It just doesn't make sense. Dave darling are you sure you've got this right?'

''Fraid so. The Banner've been ringing me from London and just now I called them back and they confirmed the story. And, oh Hell, the editor wants me back there to sniff around the sailing community although much good that'll do. This looks like a revenge attack – nothing to do with sailing.'

Josie made up her mind. 'No, we must go back as soon as possible. I want to console Lorraine – oh God, what about her little Kitty and Simon, they've lost their daddy.' She stared at him. 'Dave darling, if you can discover anything around the sailing scene that will help the law you must do it and now.'

CHAPTER 3

Emily was forced to cast her mind back to that dreadful day and the news that came in that evening. A man named Jebbs had gone to the sports hall where his ex-wife taught yoga. He carried a sports bag and in it was an automatic weapon. Where he had obtained this was uncertain although it might have come from a terrorist source. But Jebbs had not been content to kill only his ex-wife. He had killed her and then turned the gun on a huddled group of gym users, killed five and left two badly wounded including a teenager. Another woman, a well known local figure who had bravely fought him and tried to take the gun had died as well. This atrocity had not been anywhere near Emily's home but had been in a Somerset village eighty miles away. Jebbs had made no attempt to escape. He had been overpowered and held by the security staff and handed straight to the police. Emily knew that the Banner and the other tabloids were screaming for a return of the death penalty. She was unswerving in her opposition to this. Tony Travis, her mentor, was opposed and his retired clerk of chambers had witnessed two hangings in the old days. These had affected him badly. Tom also felt strongly against it. In Olifa he had witnessed a tearful group mourning the victim of a firing squad. Olifa, the friendly South American country; she had loved it. It was where she and her friends had won their Olympic medal. But it had a very dark side. She was shocked that the man who had tried to sabotage both her father's and her Olympic dreams had somehow recovered his fortune and was an occasional mansion guest not ten miles from her home.

Their friend Lorraine, who had so tragically lost her own husband, lived just down the road from them in Alresford. Emily had posted her a condolence card. Once poor Wallace's body was released there would be the ordeal of the funeral. How on earth would Lorraine and her two little children cope with that? The thought of losing her Tom made her feel sick. Well, Jebbs had paid for his crime but at the hands of a cowboy style lynch mob and not by justice in an English court. But why had these thugs killed poor Wally and the other prison officer? It didn't make sense. No doubt the police would bring more grief to the families of the Somerset murder victims.

Three days passed and the media storm had far from abated. It seemed that the police were getting nowhere and the tabloid press knew it. Emily had received a brief phone call from their bereaved friend, Lorraine thanking her for her condolence card. Lorraine had taken her children to their grandparents' home. She was quiet but controlled and Emily could only guess at the torment below the surface. Today Emily was off to Winchester Crown court for the first day of the Modlington prosecution. Tom was home catching up on his paper work and Lily had come in to look after Peter.

Emily was packing her papers into her briefcase when there came a tap on the window. She looked up in surprise to see Dave.

'Hi, what's happened to the honeymoon and where's Josie?'

'Josie's in our Bayswater flat. We had to cut the honeymoon short because the Banner have summoned me home.'

'But why? You don't have to be ruled by them.'

'This is different. It's the Sussex murders. They think there might be a sailing connection.'

Emily snorted in annoyance. 'That's crazy. And you're not going to pester poor Lorraine are you?' She glared at him.

'Oh come on, what do you take me for? Lorraine's our friend. No it's probably crap, but Wally sailed and it seems Jebbs was a photographer who did a lot of nautical stuff. He traded under the name: C-PICS.'

Emily was startled. 'Oh, that funny little man. Yes, I saw him at Hamble and some of his pictures got in the yacht mags.' She grimaced. 'He didn't seem like a psychopath.'

'He had an unfaithful wife,' Tom intervened. 'They reckon he blew a fuse.'

'So why take it out on those poor victims, you tell me that.' Emily was angry.

'Can't tell you that. I'm not a psychiatrist. But you see what I'm getting at,' said Dave. 'I thought the sailing connection was rubbish but now I think it needs checking. Look, we're involved in that game and I doubt the police have made the connection.'

'Then shouldn't you tip them off?'

'I promise anything I learn will be passed on.'

CHAPTER 4

Dave was not going to reveal that he was investigating the Jebbs murders and the man's subsequent lynching. At Hamble he was going to be just Dave the sailing magazine hack. He would listen as covertly as possible. Josie was driving down in her little car and they would go for a sail in his RS200 class dinghy. The little racing boat was in the sailing club dinghy park. Dave carried his sail bag across and began to rig her. He carried his tool bag and a briefcase, and in the latter was a photograph of him and Josie in the same dinghy, racing in Scotland. This was on the day that he had been recalled by the Banner to report on the Ollavasen murder. What he was aware of but would not reveal was that the picture was taken by Walter Jebbs of C-PICS marine photography. He had bought the picture from an agency and had never met Jebbs, nor could he have recognised him if the man was still alive. Before he and Josie had left for New Zealand Dave had scanned the image into a larger version, but when he took it to a framing shop in Southampton the shop man had thrown it back at him when he realised who the photographer had been. Jebbs was still alive at that point and awaiting trial.

It was a cold January morning by the Hamble River – a bit of a shock after the Auckland heat. He retreated into the club house changing rooms to pull on his sailing dry suit. He found another member that he knew and after the usual greetings, talk about the weather and the financial situation, Dave pointed across the water to the Warsash shore. 'Lot of building work going on over there?'

'Yes,' the other replied. 'Really run down that place was. It's the old yard that belonged to that miserable sod, Smidgin. Not really surprised someone did him in. Do we know who that was?'

Smidgin's death had been the most baffling of the four murders. Of course Dave knew who had done it, even though the name had not featured in the court charges; probably for lack of evidence.

'Nothing was ever proved,' he replied.

'Wonder if it was anything to do with the big murder the other day?'

'The man Jebbs you mean?'

His companion sniffed. 'Got what was coming to him that one, but why kill poor old Wally and that other bent screw?'

'Screw?'

'Sorry, slip of the tongue. I'm not proud of it but I did eighteen months – drink driving. My own fault entirely. Some of the guards were alright but some were sadistic bastards. They moved me to Ford open prison and that's where I ran into Smidgin.'

'What did you make of him?'

'As I said – miserable sod.'

Dave was interested now. 'Tell me, in the county jail. What did the inmates think of Wally? Was he there then?'

'Yes, but he was a quiet one. Did his job and didn't go out of his way to aggravate.' The man pulled on a buoyancy aid. 'Tell you something. After they let me back in here I met Wally and he never mentioned the nick. I even had a meal out with my girlfriend and Wally and Lorraine. No Wally was a great guy and I know what I'd like to do with the bastards who killed him.'

'What about the other prison officer?'

His companion glared. 'Yeah, Jones? My God; he was a bent screw.'

Dave laughed. 'I got a few of them when I fixed our wardrobe.'

'No, Dave. Jones wasn't a bully, but he was bent. Smuggled in dope and porno mags. They say he even brought in a couple of good time girls and set them up in a cellar. But much worse than that; rumour said Jones had been a screw in a secure unit near Bristol for holding nonce perverts. And they say Jones smuggled in little tiny girls for the nonces to play with.'

Dave was horrified. 'But that's disgusting. Why did no one deal with him?'

'Ask me something easier. I'm sorry for what happened to Wally and even hanging Jebbs was wrong, but Jones – I don't give a fuck about him.'

Dave went outside to his boat. He had made some headway in his investigation and there, in the distance, was Josie parking her car.

'How did it go?' Tom asked as Emily walked indoors. She was back from her first day prosecuting Lord Modlington.

She sighed. 'I hoped we'd get a guilty plea, but no. The old fool is stubborn and the defence are playing clever.'

'He was a top politician in his day,' Tom mused. 'Did he have a record of child abuse?'

'No, I gather the police went back twenty years, questioned a load of people and found nothing.'

19

'So, why are the defence being clever?'

Emily hung up her winter coat that had covered her smartly tailored court suit. 'Well, it seems the police had a tip-off and they went to his house and seized the discs. We were shown some of the stuff and it's really dire – total porn. Trouble is the police witness had to admit the discs were still in a shrink wrap and hadn't been accessed.'

'So, how does this Lord Modlington account for them?'

'He hasn't taken the stand yet, but I can't see us losing this one. He's far too old to be sent to prison and he's in a wheelchair so he can hardly do community service.'

'But, Em, you've got to make an example of him. Can't let a bloody politician be above the law.'

Emily grinned. 'Everybody hates politicians, I wonder why?'

'Saturday tomorrow,' said Tom. 'How say we go and look at our boat?'

'What about Peter?'

'Lily's coming with us and if it's too cold she can take him into the restaurant. They've got a kid's play room.'

CHAPTER 5

'Sorry, sir but we've drawn a blank. None of the agencies with pretend police vehicles have hired anything except to one TV company and that wasn't on the day in question.'

Sussex Chief Constable Fox was not surprised. He glanced at his Chief Superintendent sitting opposite. So serious was the mass murder that Fox needed updates by the hour. Tomorrow he was due to preside at a press conference and he had nothing constructive to say to them. 'Tell me,' he asked. 'Who might want to kill the two prison officers?'

'Well, sir, obviously former inmates with a grievance and I can tell you a bit more about that. We've had a flood of ex-cons who have come forward with views on the man Jones. He was definiteley corrupt. Someone was paying him to smuggle in drugs, and in one case, prostitutes into his jail. But it's worse. They allege he was supplying kids to that secure paedophile unit over by Bristol.'

Fox, who had heard most things in a long career, was shocked. 'For God's sake. How did he get away with that?'

'Seems he was a nasty bit of work and obviously somebody was paying and probably protecting him. The cons in the jail were buying drugs, but why give those stinking paedos their playthings?'

'Well, that could be a reason why someone wanted Jones disposed of,' Fox paused. 'Better track down some of the prisoners who were in contact with Jones. They could tell us something.'

Dave and Josie had rigged their dinghy and started sailing. It was a cold frosty day but the sun was shining and a gentle breeze blew from the east. Even though it was mid-winter the Hamble was still full of boats, far fewer than in summertime but more than a few on the moorings and in the marinas.

'Did you find anything that involved poor Wally?' Josie asked.

'No, but the other prison officer was a rotten apple.' He told her what he'd heard.

Josie adjusted her jib sheet. 'If the killers are ex-convicts, why kill both Jones and Wally?'

'I know; the jail inmates quite liked Wally. By all accounts he was fair.'

'Doesn't look as if there's a connection with sailing after all,' Josie grumbled. 'Can't we fly back and finish our honeymoon?'

Dave put his arm around her as the dinghy wobbled. 'Another two days and if I've nothing for the Banner we'll chuck it and go home to NZ.'

They were now able to relax and enjoy their sailing, working the tricky wind shifts in the river while taking in the winter scene. They returned to the club and pulled out the boat. 'Time for a cuppa I think,' said Dave.

'As long as it's nothing stronger,' Josie replied. 'We're both driving separate cars.'

In the club house they were intercepted by the secretary. 'Heard you two were back in the UK. And you're married – congratulations.' The man suddenly looked serious. 'I've just had Lorraine Markham on the phone. She's heard you were back and she would be very grateful if you would see her.'

'Oh, poor Lorraine,' said Josie. 'Yes, of course we'll see her. We'll do anything to help her won't we, Dave?'

'Of course we will. I gather she went to her parents' house, but I don't know where that is.'

'Wait a minute,' said the secretary. 'I've got it written down.' He waved them into his office. 'Yes, here we are: St John's Road in Liss.'

'Where's that?' asked Dave.

'I know it,' Josie replied. 'It's about an hour away up the M27 and A3. We'd better just take your car and I'll navigate. I'll do anything to help Lorraine at a time like this.'

In the end Dave set the address into the satnav and drove with a very subdued Josie in the passenger seat. They found the house, an upmarket bungalow in a leafy street. Lorraine's father was a doctor from Trinidad who had come to England in the 1970s and done well.

'Oh, I don't like this,' said Josie.

'I know darling. This is never easy. Just be yourself.'

Lorraine's mother welcomed them. 'I'm so glad you've come.'

'How is she?' asked Josie, 'and how are the little ones.'

The lady shook her head. 'I don't think they've fully taken it in yet, but it's such a sad thing and why for God's sake? Why kill poor Wally? He's never hurt anyone in his life.'

'Have the police told you anything?' asked Dave.

'They sent a poor girl constable round. She was sympathetic but couldn't tell us anything.'

'Oh, Lorri,' Josie rushed across the room and hugged her friend who had just come through the door.

Lorraine was a friend to both of them. She was an extrovert girl from her father's Afro-Caribbean background and English mother. She worked as a midwife in a South Coast hospital. They both knew that it was Lorraine who had presided at the birth of Emily's little Peter. She was a keen small boat sailor and had crewed for husband Wallace. Between the pair of them they had won races and club trophies. Today she looked subdued but controlled. What she was feeling below the surface Dave didn't like to think.

'Thank you so much for coming, you're such good friends.' Lorraine spoke quietly without a falter. 'Tom and Emily were here earlier and they told me you were at Hamble. By the way I'm not giving up sailing. I'll take the helm and find a crew until the kids are old enough.'

'Lorri,' asked Josie. 'How are they bearing up? It must be awful.'

Lorraine's face showed her first flicker of grief. 'We've told them that Daddy is in heaven but one day they'll see him again.' She was sobbing now.

'Oh, Lorri' I'm so sorry,' Josie hugged her again.

Lorraine wiped her eyes and then in a low voice. 'I've tried to talk to the police but I can't get through to them. Wally was very moody in the last few months. Something or someone upset him. I think it was to do with work but not all to do with work.' She broke away from Josie and began to walk around the room. 'You know that very posh yacht club just along the coast there?'

'Well, there's several,' said Dave. 'But do you mean the Royal King Henry?'

'Yes, that's the one, but I've never been there. We were plebs, and worse I'm black, or I imagine that's what they'd think.'

'We've never been there,' said Dave. 'Josie's posh but I'm an uncouth Kiwi.'

'I'll tell you what,' Lorraine was intense. 'There's some big nob in that place who knew something was going to happen to Jebbs. You see Wally didn't want to go on that trip but that slimy little creep Jones did. Neither had any connection with that Sussex prison, they just went over there with the van.'

Dave was alert now. 'Lorri, have you any idea who this man at the King Henry might be and what on earth was his connection with all this?'

'Wally was so uptight that he shouted something in his sleep. 'Jebbs-Jebbs! then he called out a name: sounded like *Great Bigarse*, but I'm not sure. But all the time Wally was nervous and he wouldn't talk about it.'

'What's the connection with the King Henry?'

'Not sure, but Wally told me that if anything funny happened: "Tell the police to look in the King Henry". Or that's what he mumbled. At first I thought it was a pub.' Suddenly she turned a tear-stained face to them both. 'Dave it was you that sussed out the Hamble murder. I hated that Ollavasen but I didn't wish him dead. I don't care about Jebbs, but Jones, excuse me, he was shit, but the police are not interested. Could you nose around and find anything?'

They stayed and had a cup of tea with Lorraine and her mother. The two children were more subdued than normal but still played happily. They said their farewells. 'Lorri' I'll listen and see if I can hear anything. I'm a journalist and that's what we're good at.' Dave gave the girls a supportive hug.

Outside he turned to Josie. 'Sorry, Darling, but we can't get back honeymooning for a week or so. Tomorrow I'm off to the Banner head office and talk to the crime boss.'

Josie looked disappointed. 'You've learned something?'

'Oh, yes. You see the Rear Commodore of the King Henry is. Graham Blake-Grass. You get it *Great Big Arse*. That's what Lorri' heard. I'd wager on it. So I'm going to find all I can about the man.'

CHAPTER 6

Tom turned the Renault through the gate of Bingham's boat yard. It was here that their new family sailing cruiser was laid up for the winter. He parked and he and Emily climbed out. They were alone now having left Lily and Peter at the warm restaurant. A cold breeze wafted across the water and with it a few flakes of snow.

Emily stood back and admired the little yacht. *'White Petunia'*, that's a silly name. Do we have to stick with it?'

'No, but they used to say it was unlucky to change a ship's name – doesn't worry me. You're the one that's all into religion and superstition.'

'Not in this case. Let's change it to just *Petunia*.'

Tom found a ladder and they climbed aboard. 'Gosh, look at that place along there. What is it?' asked Emily.

'That's Magnum Millennium Marine, they build super-yachts; like floating hotels. Earn two million and we'll have one.'

'That'll be the day – and anyway who wants a gin palace when we can sail.'

'Dave was asking about a man who has one of those. That might be the boat we can see.'

Emily took another look at the super-yacht. 'I told Dave to talk to my Dad. He's a member of the King Henry, although he doesn't go there much except for business.'

They climbed all over the little Hunter 21, a smaller version of the twenty-seven footer that Emily's parents sailed from Chichester, and the same class as owned by Tom's father, the older Peter. Tom moved around noting every detail on a note pad. 'I think we'll renew the standing rigging,' he said. 'Chris the rigger says he can make up the stays in his Chichester shop and the yard here will fit them.'

Emily was checking the tiny cabin. 'Cooker looks OK,' she said. 'Seems like they've put the gas cylinder in the anchor well and that's pretty safe.' Tom knew she was remembering the awful time when those mad people who later abducted her had tried to destroy her parents' boat with a sabotaged gas cylinder. 'Can't see the outboard motor,' she added.

'The yard say it's knackered,' Tom called. 'But they've got a nice four-stroke unit at the shop in Warsash.'

'I suppose so,' Emily sounded uncertain. 'That was Smidgin's place.'

'I know but things move on. There's a new owner now – nothing like Smidgin.'

Emily grunted. 'Who is that man Dave was asking about?'

'I've never met him. I don't move in those circles, but he's Graham Blake-Grass. Billionaire business tycoon as you would expect with a boat like that. He's not much respected. The locals really do call him Bigarse.'

'So, is that his yacht over there?'

'Dunno, but I read that he owns a Magnum sixty footer.'

'I can't tell you too much,' said Steve. 'I know the man he's a shareholder in Easterbroke Sails but he doesn't use us. He's a power boater.'

Dave and Josie had rung ahead and arranged to meet Emily's father, Steve Simpson at his Sussex home. Both of them knew the Simpson family, not only Emily and her young brother, but Steve and Emily's mother Kirsten had, with themselves, witnessed the terrible but poignant, ending of the long trail from the original Ollavasen murder. Steve Simpson the double Olympic and Paralympic gold medallist was an icon in the sailing world. He ran the sailmaking business with branches in five countries presided over by his wife. Kirsten had inherited the firm and Steve provided the technical expertise. Following his Olympic and then Paralympic achievements an enthusiastic nation had elevated this quiet reclusive sportsman to a knighthood. Emily's match racing Olympic gold had brought the family's tally to three. Emily had been given an MBE along with her crewmates; not that she ever boasted or even mentioned this.

'Why this interest in Blake-Grass?' asked Steve.

Dave explained what he had learned from Lorraine.

'Yes, Blake-Grass is obscenely wealthy,' said Steve. 'He's done big property deals in New York. I believe he owns a brewery here and television stations in South America.'

'Is there a New Zealand connection? It's a funny thing but that name rings a bell and I can't remember why.' Dave shook his head.

'More than likely: the man's got a finger in many pies worldwide. But that's his secret, I guess.'

'I'm due to talk to the Banner's crime editor tomorrow,' said Dave. 'He'll likely know if this Grass is into anything shady.'

'Can't see why there's a connection to that ghastly business the other day, or to the slaughter in Somerset.'

'It's the sailing connection,' said Dave. 'That's why the Banner hired me. Jebbs was involved in sailing and poor Wally was a good racing helm and after what Lorraine said I'm bound to follow that up.'

'Hmm,' Steve leaned forward and put more logs on the sitting room fire. 'There's a reception at the Royal King Henry next week. Blake-Grass is their rear commodore. We weren't going but after what you've said I think we will and take the temperature. Kirsten can listen to the ladies.'

'Listen to who?' Kirsten had entered the room and Steve explained.

'Good, I don't like that man,' she said. 'That time last year he sat next to me and tried to lift my skirt.'

Steve laughed. 'At your age, girl, you should be flattered.'

CHAPTER 7

Graham Blake-Grass stood still while he admired his super-yacht, *Conqueror*. She was a beauty and better, she never let him down. Not like a bloody woman, they always seemed to turn sour on him. He had just passed his sixtieth birthday. Things really were at last going well. He had cleared the air with his personal problems and that felt most satisfactory. And no one could touch him now. He was who he was: the generous donor to both the Tory Party and the US Republicans. Wasn't he patron to seven charities? Yes, he had wiped the slate clean and he felt safe now. That stupid girl of his was far too nosy and he needed to show that he controlled his world. This evening he was hosting his latest cocktail party aboard *Conqueror*. Members of the Royal King Henry would attend as well as the local mayor and MP. That yacht racer Stephen Simpson had also accepted the invitation. That fellow needed cutting down to size; a knighthood for God's sake to the son born to a pub landlady. The man had never been to a decent school and had once been a footballer. Well, the fellow had given that up to go sailing little boats and winning Olympics. Blake-Grass had never sailed a dinghy and had no wish to.

He had been badly treated as a young man. A prefect at a top public school he had been expelled for getting the house master's au pair girl in trouble. Yes, little Olga and her brats, the source of all his recent problems. He wondered how many little children around the world could claim him as father. Anyway time to go aboard and fetch out his designer dinner suit.

Emily found Peter and Lily playing a game with a string of beads. Her lovely boy was such a happy child. Sometimes he cried but more often he laughed. How she longed to make a brother, or better still, a sister for him.

'You been a good boy?' she gave him a cuddle.

'Oh, yes,' said Lily. 'He never gets bored. We've had a great time haven't we.' The little boy smiled. 'How was your new yacht?' she asked.

Tom laughed, 'Yacht is pushing it a bit. *Petunia's* only a little cruiser. We'll take you out on her come the summer.'

'Not sure about that. My Kev was in the Navy and I went on his ship a couple of times, but that was a big'un and safe in dock.'

'We'll see,' said Emily. 'I'm hungry. Come on, let's eat.'

They went into the dining room and stood looking at the menu selection written up on a blackboard.

'Hi there, Emily', the voice was their friend, the manageress. 'Have you seen the Echo today? It's all about you prosecuting that dirty old lord.'

'Really, I saw they had a reporter.'

'Dirty old sod. I hope you get him sent down for a long stretch.'

Emily laughed. 'I think the disgrace will be the punishment. Anyway we haven't finished the trial.'

'Have you seen poor Wally's wife? I feel awful; you know they were eating here only a week ago.' Jane looked around the room and dropped her voice to an intense whisper. 'He was very uptight about something. Could he have had a premonition – isn't that what it's called?'

'Yes, that's what it's called. But I guess some of it was to do with the trip he was due to make.'

'Look I don't eavesdrop on customers, you know that. But Wally was angry and I heard him say something funny, or not funny, he was angry.'

'Can you tell us?' asked Tom.

'He said; "Jebbs – we know someone put him up to it and I can have a pretty good guess who Jones is".'

'Have you told the police?' asked Tom.

'Yes, we called their special line and told them but I don't think it made much impression.'

They gave their order and found a table. Emily rummaged in her bag and to out Peter's soft food. 'I think we'd better tell Dave what she just said.'

'Yes, I agree, but it doesn't mean the crimes have a sailing connection. That's what Dave's been asked to find.'

Steve and Kirsten parked the car at the Magnum-Millennium marina. Steve stared at their destination. *Conqueror* was not a yacht, she was definitely a ship. They walked towards the floodlit gangway. Both had attended functions at the gaudiest of the world's yacht clubs and were too blasé to be intimidated by this gin palace as the term went. A stream of expensively dressed guests was heading towards the gangway and they followed. Steve was in no way envious, but he felt annoyed to witness this ostentatious display of vulgar wealth when only a mile away there were families struggling to raise enough money to pay a mortgage and feed their children.

They mounted the carpeted gangway and entered the enveloping warmth of the ship. The place was already full of partygoers and Steve looked around to see if there was anyone he knew. He wasn't sure whether to laugh or not when they were intercepted by a character in full evening attire with a red sash. He was tall, baby bald with a broken nose and chronically obese. Steve could just see traces of a lurid tattoo of a snake on his neck. 'Ladies and gentlemen,' this comic major-domo roared. 'Sir Stephen and Lady Simpson.'

Now they could see Blake-Grass hand outstretched with a broad smile advancing on them. With him was a girl at least thirty years younger. 'Sir Stephen,' Blake-Grass gripped his hand. 'We are honoured to have a famous racing yachtsman with us tonight.' He then introduced the girl as his wife, Cerise. Not for the first time Steve found himself almost, but not quite, liking this character. The blonde Cerise took charge of Kirsten and her coat and pointed out the cloakroom.

The yacht's huge saloon was crowded with smartly dressed guests, none of whom they really knew. The Royal King Henry Yacht Club was a yacht club with a capital Y. In reality it was a gathering place for city brokers and others to meet in a more sociable atmosphere than day-to-day. Competition or racing sailing was not really on the agenda. Steve paid the exorbitant annual membership fee with some reluctance, but he knew that even if these tycoons did little real yachting they liked to sponsor long distance events and such things as America's Cup challenges. And that led to prestige orders for sails.

This had also triggered the Ollavasen murder and all the grief to which that had led. They could not forget that. Even as these thoughts entered his head he saw across the saloon that ghastly character Hengist Crickerman. Crickerman had been suspected by the police in the Ollavasen case but had narrowly escaped being murdered himself. But at least the man was a yachtsman who had skippered his own yacht.

Now Crickerman was grinning and waving to him. Steve was still limping from the stroke and was careful not to trip on the soft carpeting. 'Hello, Steve, mate,' Crickerman shook hands with the same heartiness as their host. 'How's your little girl?'

'Emily's fine and doing well in her profession.'

'Yeah, she prosecuting old Ferdy Modlington.' Crickerman's Australian accent was vivid now as it dropped to a level Steve found hard to hear. 'Poor old Ferdy. Hope she goes a bit easy. We reckon he was set up.'

'Well, that's up to the court now,' Steve was wary.

'Yeah, let's hope the truth comes out.' Crickerman's voice returned to its normal pitch. 'What you think of the Jebbs killing?'

'I would call it a lynching. I don't know about your country, Mr Crickerman, but we don't do lynchings here. We're more concerned about the prison officer who was murdered. He was a friend of my daughter and son-in-law.'

Crickerman nodded, 'Yeah, sorry to hear that of course. That's the guy who did a bit of your little dinghy stuff?'

'Yes, with his wife. They were useful.'

'Well,' Crickerman continued. 'My London neighbours are the scummy Daily Banner. You can imagine what they've been making of that business.'

Steve grinned. 'Not my usual reading.'

'Nor mine, mate. I was going to sue them over the Ollavasen business, but my lawyers said I'd only lose and blow a lot of good money and that's something I never do.'

I bet you don't, thought Steve. Kirsten had now come to his rescue. 'Mr Crickerman, my daughter Emily met your wife in New Zealand.'

'Eh? Ex-wife; I discarded her – mouthy bitch.'

Kirsten smiled in a way Steve knew too well. 'Emily says she was charming.'

'I bet she was. What was she doing in NZ? They're Kiwis – sheep shaggers – waste of space.'

'She was at the wedding of some mutual friends.'

They left Crickerman glowering into his champagne glass. Now Steve saw a man he really did know. Sam Pollingham, the eccentric power boat designer who did freelance work for Magnum. Pollingham was an erratic, untidy, unpredictable character and typically the only male guest not wearing black tie. He was dressed in a rather shabby dark lounge suit, a change from his standard daytime attire of white overalls.

'Hello, Sam,' said Steve. 'Fancy seeing you here. Now, if I have to make a guess I would say it was you that designed this gin palace.'

Sam grinned. 'True, and Steve: sell that sail making outfit and I've a notion you could have one of these too.'

'Oh yes, big laugh. And how would we find the yard fees?'

Steve and Kirsten circulated and met more people they didn't know, and Kirsten drank more champagne than she intended. Steve as driver had to be more cautious. The odd incident came as the proceedings were winding down. Cerise Blake-Grass had fetched their winter coats, To Steve she was a pretty girl. Although he wasn't envious he supposed an oligarch like Blake-Grass could have a pick of lovely nubile girls.

'Please, Sir Stephen,' Cerise had a pleading look.

'Oh Cerise,' Steve replied. 'Don't bother with the Sir. I'm Steve.'

She smiled. 'Steve, please, did your daughter know Wallace Markham?'

'Yes, but all the Hamble dinghy set knew Wallace and Lorraine. What happened was terrible. All their friends are feeling sick about it,'

Cerise had a look of pain. 'It's just that I heard something and I don't like it.'

CHAPTER 8

'Hey, someone looks pleased with themselves.' Tom laughed.

'Well, so I should be. We won. Guilty verdict and substantial fine.'

'Well I suppose so, but I feel a bit sorry for that poor old bloke. I mean at his age he wouldn't be able to actually do anything, sex-wise that is.'

Emily laughed. 'Let's see how good at it you are at eighty something. It's an odd thing. I was beginning to think our case was slipping away. The defence were making such a big deal of the discs being still wrapped. But it didn't mean that the old fellow wasn't waiting for when he could unwrap them and start slobbering over them.'

'I've had a pretty good day as well,' he grinned. 'I'm going to be regional controller and a ten percent pay rise.'

'Oh yes, then we can afford child number two.'

'Well, I'm not sure about that.'

Emily stood up and confronted her husband. 'From tonight I'm off the pill. It's your choice. Make a baby or no sex.'

Tom smiled weakly. 'That seems a no win situation.'

'To you maybe. To me it's win-win all the way.' She picked up and cuddled Peter. 'You'd like a little brother or sister wouldn't you?'

The Daily Banner's chief crime correspondent was a dour journalist of many years experience who had grown up in the shadow of the famous, and sometimes infamous, Sid Everett. Dave had known Sid and seen him in action although he could never follow the man's ruthless methods in pursuit of a story. After all, Dave was a sports journalist even though he had gained huge prestige through the Ollavasen affair.

'Hi, Dave, come on in and sit down. How was the wedding to your lovely Josie?'

'It was great and Josie's got another book coming out soon. But that's not why you wanted to see me.'

'Yeah, quite right. Your downunder philosophy eh? Cut the crap and tell it as it is.'

Dave grinned. 'Something like that.'

'Right, any connection with Blake-Grass? Well, yes there is one but I doubt it's significant. Eileen Jebbs the teacher and ex-wife was we think – wait for it – a bastard daughter of B-G. I've got people working on that.'

Dave felt disappointment. 'That would be a tragedy for him wouldn't it?'

'You'd think so and anyway we've no connection between him and Jebbs apart from some pictures Jebbs shot of B-Gs big yacht. But they were all agency work and commissioned by the ship's builder.'

'Jebbs is dead,' said Dave. 'And he's no loss even though I don't care for lynching. But the prison officer, Wally Markham. He was a friend of ours and we sailed against him and his wife. She's told us there was something troubling him and he called out Blake-Grass's name in his sleep.'

The crime chief frowned. 'There's a puzzle there. Why did the service use a prison van from Hampshire to fetch a con from Lewes jail in Sussex?'

'Lorraine says that happens quite a bit. The prison vans are run by a commercial firm.'

'Yes, but your friend Markham was Hampshire and so was the other man, Jones. My sources say Jones was under investigation for corruption.'

'That's right,' said Dave. 'By all accounts he was an evil bastard. Shouldn't have been guarding a jail – should've been an inmate himself.'

'Yes, Jones had an odd background for a prison officer. He was a posh public school type. Can't find out too much about B-G. He's made billions in property deals in the U.S. and South America. He owns a computer software company here and a brewery plus investments in China.'

Dave intervened. 'I heard that name in New Zealand but I can't remember the context.'

'Ah, there I can help you. Blake-Grass has a mining concession in your South Island and he got it by dubious means. Or rather he donated half a million dollars to charities.'

The telephone shrilled. 'The crime chief picked it. 'Hello Max, what's up? Bloody hell! Talk of the devil. Max, find out all you can and then email me a report A.S.A.P.'

He replaced the receiver and stared at Dave. 'Blake-Grass has been found dead in his yacht.'

CHAPTER 9

Emily and Tom had been startled to find the entrance to the village sealed off by police tape and stern looking constables in reflecting yellow jackets. For Emily this was a reprise of that day near her parents' home. 'Please, what's happened?'

'There has been a serious incident and we must ask you to turn round and go elsewhere.'

Oh for God's sake, thought Tom. Why do coppers always talk like this? 'Please we only want to look at our boat in the yard down there.'

'Sorry, sir, but not today I'm afraid. There's been an incident.'

'Not at the seafront boatyard. That's where we wanted to go.'

'No, sir, but the incident is on this road and you can't go down here today.'

Tom was beginning to be angry, and at this moment Emily, typically sensing this intervened. 'Constable, of course we'll turn round but can we go the other side of the river?' She gave the man a sweet smile.

'Oh, Miss,' the man straightened and Tom almost felt he was about to salute. 'Miss, you're the lawyer aren't you?'

'Well, yes, that's my job.'

'You put away that dirty old lord. I was on court watch that day. Got what he deserved we say.'

'Thank you.'

The copper had suddenly relaxed and lowered his voice. 'You could have another one now. The dead man is that Blake-Grass. It's Magnum Millennium we've sealed off.'

This on top of everything that had happened in the last ten days was a real shock. Neither of them knew the man, but Emily's parents had met him only forty eight hours ago. 'Is it a suspicious death then?' she asked.

'Can't tell you that, but forensics are there. Can't tell you more.'

They turned around and then Tom rang Steve and Kirsten.

Dave had driven straight to find Josie in their Bayswater flat. 'I'm sorry, darling, but things are getting out of hand. I can't jack in this investigation now. The paper is relying on me.'

Josie put her arms around him and kissed him. 'You're a sports journalist. Why can't they let you do that instead of all this crime stuff?'

'It's the sea and yacht connection. That's why they need me. If it wasn't for poor Lorraine I'd tell the Banner to take jump. But for her sake I've got to follow this one.'

'Do you know for certain this man's been murdered? He could have had an accident.'

'If that's the case, OK ; but that man knew something. Lorraine thinks so and I called Steve Simpson at his office and he agrees. He says Blake-Grass's wife was worried. He reckons she knew something about Wally, but the party they were at was too public. My Banner boss says the girl Jebbs killed, the ex-wife, may be an illegitimate daughter of B-G himself. Too many coincidences in my reckoning. And it's a bit odd, Bigarse must be sixty and the murdered woman teacher was mid-forties. If she was Bigarse's daughter he and her mother must have been at it as teenagers.'

Josie stood up. She grinned. 'And when did you start? Right, I'm coming with you.'

Chief Superintendent Hollins shivered as he stared at the oily waters around the *Conqueror*. It was growing dark and he had no envy for the police frogmen combing the shallow bottom of the dock. Graham Blake-Grass's body had been found floating beneath the surface near the flat stern bathing platform. He was dead, the back of his head smashed to pulp. Forensic officers had combed the yacht below and above decks. This had been no accident, a pool of congealed blood was found on the soft carpet at the foot of a stairwell and small droplets were on the stairs and across the deck to the ship's rail. The wound was brutal and could never be the result of a fall. No, this man was murdered: how and by whom, would have to wait. Hollins was not entirely surprised. Blake-Grass, one of the world's wealthiest men, would have enemies. He sighed. They would have to hold a press conference tomorrow. He had no useful information and the hacks would know it.

He turned and looked up as he heard a yell from the loud hailer in the police RIB that was patrolling the fifty metre exclusion zone. A tiny sailing dinghy had encroached into the security area in the fading light and was heading straight for *Conqueror*. The RIB was in hot pursuit of the dinghy. Hollins let out a groan half frustration and half amusement. Of all the bloody cheek, but that man knew the yacht scene. Bloody press-reporter maybe, but he knew these snooty yachties, whereas their world was a blank for Hollins himself.

'Mr Manning,' he called. 'May I ask what you are doing here, or perhaps I don't need two guesses.'

CHAPTER 10

Jasmine Harris-Evans had been woken at two o'clock in the morning by a frantic ringing of her front door bell. She prodded her slumbering husband with no result. With a sigh she slipped out of the bed and made her way downstairs. She was nervous now – this didn't make sense. Was it a joker or something more sinister? At least the front door was held with a security chain and there was a voice call microphone as well.

'Who is it?' she called. There came no reply. Jasmine called again and louder. Now she thought she heard a faint moan. No choice now, she opened the door a crack and called again. A limp figure was leaning against the door frame. Was this some drunk? Then a face lifted in front of her inches away.

Jasmine gasped. 'Cerise, for God's sake what's happened? Come inside at once.'

Her sister staggered over the threshold and collapsed on the floor. Cerise' face was blotched and her makeup smeared. Jasmine helped her to her feet and steered her to the settee in the sitting room.

Cerise was mumbling. 'Graham's dead. I think someone's killed him.'

'Alright, Mr Manning. I suppose I'll have to let you come aboard, or is onboard the right term?' Hollins was grinning now.

Dave was relieved. He knew that this intrusion by water was more than cheeky. It was just the sort of thing Sid Everett would have tried and probably got himself arrested.

'Either term is all right,' he grinned back in reply. 'Can my wife come aboard as well?'

'Yes, but I must warn you that things have happened here that might upset the lady.'

'I doubt it,' said Dave. 'Josie's a tough nut. She's been a reporter as well. She covered that big train disaster a year back – dead bodies everywhere.'

'Please can I?' pleaded Josie. 'It's freezing cold sitting in this dinghy.'

Dave began to hand the dinghy round to the stern bathing platform. Hollins glared at him. 'No, Mr Manning, not the back of the boat. It's a crime scene.'

They waited a minute while a white overall-clad policeman lowered a boarding ladder.

Dave gave Josie a hand up and then followed to the deck of the super-yacht.

'Mr Hollins, the rear of a ship is the stern not the back.'

'All right, Mr Manning. I know I've worked this area for twenty years and I suppose it's time I picked up some of your yachtie jargon.'

Dave looked around impressed by the size and scope of this ship, and ship she was: vast, slick and polished from bow to stern. 'So, the stern is your crime scene?'

'Mr Manning, that is not for information until the press conference.'

Dave thought for a moment. Even in their dry suits they were feeling cold. 'Mr Hollins. What if we give you some info that might help?'

'Go ahead.'

'Wallace Markham was our friend. We've talked in confidence to Lorraine, his widow. Wally was really troubled about something and Lorraine said it was connected to Blake-Grass. Seems he called out about Jebbs in his sleep and then mentioned Blake-Grass. What he called was actually "big arse", but that's what the man was called behind his back. Then the chief crime reporter on the Banner has found out that the ex-wife that Jebbs killed could be Big Arse's daughter.'

'Very well,' said Hollins. 'I note what you say.'

'I'll tell you some more. Steve Simpson, who you know, was at the big party held onboard here. He said that Big Arse's wife was upset and knew something about our Wally but didn't say what because there were too many people around.'

Hollins now looked interested. 'In due course we will talk to Mrs Blake-Grass, but thank you for that at least.'

'Look,' said Dave. 'If you hold a press conference you'll have to give the details. If it was foul play how was he topped?'

'I suppose so. If you must know, our official reply is that there was an implosion to the back of the skull by a heavy instrument.'

'That sounds politically correct cop-speak. Who did it, his missus?'

'We are not in a position to comment but we will question many people and we rule nothing in and nothing out. However, thank you for the information you have given me and if we proceed further with it we may need you to give us an official statement.'

That was that. Dave knew not to push further. It was dark now with little breeze and he was grateful that Hollins released his guard RIB to tow them in their dinghy to the sailing club on the opposite shore.

CHAPTER 11

Jasmine sat with an arm around her younger sister and watched as Cerise sipped a cup of strong coffee. 'Oh, Jaz ... she sobbed. Someone's killed Graham and I didn't see anything. He's in the sea floating...' Now Cerise howled and bent her head to the table top.

'Shall I ring the police?' asked Jasmine.

'I rang them and then I ran.'

Jasmine gave up at this point, but she went into the office and dialled treble nine.

She was at her most persuasive and in the end the emergency medical callout agreed to visit.

'Hey. What's going on?' The voice was Ifor, her husband. He had found his way downstairs and was sleepily rubbing his eyes.

Jasmine was cautious. Ifor and Cerise did not get on. Jasmine knew all her husband's faults only too well but she could never understand his hostility to her sister, nor Cerise' to him.

'Cerise has had a nasty shock, so Ifor please be sensible and not make things worse.'

'What shock? That woman's got an overworked imagination.'

Jasmine walked closer and dropped her voice. 'She says Graham has died.'

'Has he now. Well she'll inherit a good heap of loot.'

'Ifor, no, that's not what this is about.' Jasmine was angry now. Why the hell had she ever married this insensitive brute? But he was manly and great value in bed.

The night doctor arrived half an hour later. He was a courteous Anglo-Indian who apologised for taking so long to reach them. A drunk had fallen on his face in the nearby town. They took the doctor to the spare bedroom where Cerise had been put and Jasmine waited nervously outside the door. After twenty minutes the doctor reappeared.

'She's in a bad state of shock. With your permission I think we will move her to hospital.'

Jasmine was shocked. 'Surely she's not that bad.'

'You tell me her husband has died. Do you know the circumstances?'

'If it's true it seems it was a violent death but we don't know what happened.'

The doctor thought for a moment. 'Her blood pressure is far too high and her heart rate has me worried. There's something not quite right and I would advise having her into full care for twenty-four hours.'

'All right,' Jasmine felt relieved.

'I am also concerned,' the doctor added. 'There are stains on her skin and clothes that lo to me like human blood. I cannot confirm anything myself of course, but the hospital will.'

'Well, that wasn't any hardship was it?' Emily grinned at her husband as he sat up in bed gazing sleepily back at her.

'No, and I agree you're right. Peter could do with a sibling.'

Emily having abandoned her contraceptive precautions was ready to have a second pregnancy. Tom, reluctant at first, had gradually come round to the idea.

'As long as it doesn't muck up your career,' he muttered

Emily laughed, in fact she felt a little bit light headed. She was fairly confident that she was at maximum fertility and that the last two nights shenanigans would do the business. 'Did you hear the phone ring?'

'No, when?'

'Dave rang. Would you believe it but he and Josie sailed across the river right up to the Bigarse yacht and the cops let them on board.'

'So it was murder.'

'Very much so. Very traditional: battering with a blunt instrument.'

'Do the police know who did it?'

'Dave spoke to Superintendent Hollins, you remember him?'

'Oh yeah, bit of a plod. It was Dave who put them onto the Ollavasen murderer.'

'Well Dave suspects they are zeroing in on B-Gs wife. She's younger than him and has a reputation for being erratic.'

'In that case, they're probably a mile off course.'

'Where is this woman?' asked Hollins.

'She's on our territory, sir,' replied the young girl PC. 'She's in the Queen Alexandra hospital.'

'Do we know how that came about?'

'It seems she sought refuge in her sister's house – that's in the countryside near East Meon. The hospital say she was admitted suffering from severe shock.'

Yes, thought Hollins. A woman who has just killed her husband would be in shock. He hoped she would be less in shock this morning because she was about to have bedside visit from the CID.

That next morning Dave rang the office of Sam Pollingham. Sam was a yacht designer, in fact a most prestigious designer. A former top rugby player and boxer, Sam was a burly if slightly overweight guy and not somebody one would like to mess with. It was Sam who had designed the super-yacht *Conqueror*. Dave had met Sam Pollingham but didn't know him too well. Once he would have blenched at intruding like this. It seemed he was beginning to become a little bit like old Sid Everett.

'Morning, David,' Sam sounded mildly sleepy. 'I suppose you're trawling around for stuff about old Bigarse.'

'Hey, he died on your yacht. You don't sound as if you liked him.'

'Not my yacht,' Sam laughed. 'I've a design brief for them and sometimes I can take a trip in one but own one? I don't think so.'

'Please Mr Pollingham. I don't want to intrude. I'm a sailing journalist not a tabloid hack. But this has happened on my watch and I might be able to help the law.'

'Look,' said Sam. 'I don't know the facts, but I've an idea one of the crew was aboard that night. He's Darren Ternby. I've a notion that the police are already giving him a hard time so he may not want to talk to you.'

'Isn't he the guy who maintains the diesels?'

'Yes, the engine room man. I've an idea he didn't like Bigarse either. He kept regarding Darren as an oily rag pleb.'

Dave wondered. An engineer adapt with heavy spanners and wrenches. Could his overbearing and pompous boss have insulted him once too often? His phone was warbling so Dave pulled it out and answered.

'Been a development,' it was the Banner's crime chief. 'The cops have arrested the Blake-Grass wife. She's detained for questioning.'

'I thought they might pick on her but I do wonder. She's a tiny girl and the battering her husband to would have needed some strength.'

The Banner man laughed, but there was no humour in it. 'Women can do anything if it's a fit of passion. We would still like you to listen around for anything you can pick up about the Jebbs killing.'

CHAPTER 12

It was a cold frost-ridden Friday morning and already a blanket of snow had whitened the summit of the Downs behind the Simpson house. Steve yawned and stared out of the window. His leg, long weakened by the stroke, was always at its worst first thing in the morning. He was seventy-two years old. So many of his friends and contemporaries had retired and he didn't really envy them. He had been a sailmaker and a racing helmsman all his life. He would never sail in top competition again. The Paralympic gold medal, won against the odds, had been the culmination of his racing career. But sailmaking had been his life and the new technology and cloths fascinated him. He was not in a mood to retire just yet.

Thank goodness the road to Chichester was open again. The prison van and the tractor had long ago been removed, although groups of bad-taste voyeurs had stopped to examine the tree branch from which the lynch noose had been strung. The news of the Blake-Grass alleged murder had been a bad shock. Only a little over forty-eight hours before he and Kirsten had been at the yacht club function aboard Blake-Grass's yacht. There was something odd about that party, or at least the end of it. Wallace Markham had mentioned Blake-Grass not long before he was killed and then Blake-Grass's wife had muttered something about Wally that she couldn't mention in public. According to the television the wife, Cerise, was being detained for questioning. Somehow he couldn't see that petite little girl as a husband murderer, but then who could tell. Kirsten and he had agreed that they should contact the police with the information they knew. He would give Fox and the Sussex police a call as soon as he reached the office.

'Let's get this straight,' Chief Inspector Marchway glared at the shrunken figure across the interview room table. He must resist the temptation to feel sorry for this girl when it seemed more and more likely that she was a violent murderer. The dead husband might have been a pompous bastard, but that was not the point. 'Let's get this straight, Mrs Blake-Grass. You say you were asleep aboard the yacht and that you heard nothing until you found your husband in the water.'

The girl sobbed and nodded.

44

'We'll register that as an affirmative,' Marchway addressed the recording machine. The solicitor sat beside the girl but had so far not intervened.

'Right, let's get down to basics. Were there troubles in your marriage?'

'Chief Inspector,' said the solicitor. 'That is not an appropriate question.'

'Please,' said Marchway. 'We are trying to get to the truth of what happened.'

'No,' Cerise Blake-Grass whispered. 'No, Graham was kind. It's just...just that he knew something about that Jebbs man and the two prison warders. Could that have got him killed?' Her head sagged to the table and she sobbed. 'I loved him, he was kind.'

'Please, Chief Inspector,' said the lawyer. 'I think you've questioned enough.'

'All right,' Marchway replied. 'Interview terminated at sixteen thirty-five.' He addressed his suspect. 'I am afraid Mrs Blake-Grass that you are remanded in custody while we apply to the magistrates for two days to question you.'

Then we will charge you and put you away for life, he thought. It's her all right. She must have done it. After all we can't place anyone else near the scene that night.

Jasmine was horrified. The idea that Cerise would try and hurt Graham was ridiculous.

She would never touch him, she adored the man. It had nothing to do with his huge wealth; Cerise had always been drawn to domineering people. Ifor, Jasmine's husband didn't like Cerise and had a low opinion of Graham. Ifor had a successful business that he had built from small beginnings. For that matter she wasn't sure she liked Ifor's family. They were very Welsh and overly religious. She guessed that she was too modern and dress conscious for their liking. It was no good asking Ifor for help and sympathy. He had already declared poor Cerise to be guilty. What could she do? Yes, someone, she couldn't remember who had told her that if authority won't listen alert the press. That would mean a tabloid and that tabloid would be the Daily Banner. Not her taste of breakfast reading but it was sensational and hadn't it played a part in solving that murder in the yacht harbour. And Ifor's family didn't like the Banner. Script of Satan they would probably think. Well good!

45

'Dave,' called the Banner editor. 'There a Mrs Jasmine Harris-Evans, she's the sister of Cerise Blake-Grass. She wants to talk to us. We've checked her out and her husband runs a chain of yacht shops, so it's very much your territory.'

Dave sighed. This was becoming a bit boring. 'Josie and me want to finish our honeymoon.'

'I know, I know, but you're our contact in this world and I can say that my chief is thinking of a healthy pay-out to you if you stick with this.'

Dave rang off and then called Josie. 'Sorry, darling but I don't think I can get out of this.' He told her about the promised pay-out.

She sounded cheerful. 'Never mind, we need the money. I don't think this little flat will be big enough when we have the baby. We've talked about a cottage in the country just like Tom and Emily's.'

Dave felt relieved. 'Even with a mortgage that will cost a bomb, but I agree.'

The Harris-Evans house was just outside the Hampshire village of East Meon and it exuded wealth. The name Harris-Evans rang a distinct bell. It was Harris-Evans who had bought the run-down engine repair shop from the man Smidgin and it must be the same man who ran four yacht chandlers along the south coast. Jasmine Harris-Evans opened the front door. She would be an attractive early middle-aged woman were she not in such an obviously distressed state. 'Oh, please come in Mr Manning. You're my last hope.'

She was crying now; not false dramatics. This was genuine. 'Please, Mr Manning, my sister never hurt anyone in her life. She wouldn't even kill a mouse when we were young.'

Dave spoke as reassuringly as he knew. 'Mrs Harris-Evans, tell me what you know and I'll see if we can help you.'

CHAPTER 13

Darren Ternby was frightened and he had not been so alarmed since childhood. His boss was dead, brutally murdered and he Darren should have been around to stop that happening. He was supposed to have slept aboard the yacht *Conqueror* but he had abandoned his post to go out on the town with his girlfriend. Graham Bigarse was a good boss and he paid well. Now he was gone and the yacht would be sold. That night he had reluctantly left Carrie at her flat and then staggered back to the yacht on foot. As he came close he had heard little Cerise howling and wailing. The yacht's security lights were burning and he could see the girl swaying about on the stern bathing platform. Then she had turned and ran into the main saloon. Darren had stepped onto the stern platform and he had seen the opaque pool of what could be blood on the surface of the water. He knew in that he should have followed Cerise and ask her what had happened, but then he had blatantly chickened out. He had had a bad feeling about this. He had walked away, but as he did so he had seen another figure crouched unnaturally by the little dockside lifting crane. The man had quickly turned away but Darren knew him and wondered what he, of all the unlikely people, was doing hanging around the site at this time of night. The next day he had discovered that their boss was dead, violently battered and that the police were questioning Cerise.

Dave had to accept that the sailing connection in the whole of this nasty business was too transparent to be ignored. But he'd heard enough to be fairly certain that Cerise was not the murderer. What was more every direction he looked seemed to be connected with the Jebbs murder. It seemed unlikely that the police had made the same connection. The man Hollins was breathtakingly ignorant of all things yachting. Much as Dave regretted the loss of his time with Josie in New Zealand, this mystery involved Wally and Lorraine: his and Josie's friends. He climbed into his car and took the road for Gosport and once again to the drawing office of Sam Pollingham.

Sam was not really Dave's perception of a boffin. He was a burly character who had once been a county standard rugby player. He had left university with a science degree but had served an apprenticeship with a yacht design office in America. Sam always said his preference was for sailing yachts and he had designed four successful cruising boats, but it was Magnum Millennium who had hooked him with the big bucks and Dave felt; who could blame him. Sam was a convivial but erratic character, seen around yacht club bars and local pubs. Dave knew that Sam was not greatly fond of old Bigarse, however well the man paid him.

'Sorry, forgot to say last time. Heard you've just got spliced,' said Sam grinning. 'Congratulations.'

'Thanks, but we've had to break off the honeymoon. My paper wants me to investigate the sailing aspect of the Jebbs killing. That's why I'm being a nuisance.'

They paused while Sam's female PA came in with a tray of coffee cups. Dave took his gratefully.

'I never knew Jebbs,' said Sam. 'But he was a maniac killer and we're well rid of him.'

'But my wife and I were friends of Wallace Markham. He never hurt anyone.'

'I know,' Sam replied. 'I never met him, but I've heard he sailed near here.'

'Can you tell me anything about Blake-Grass or his wife?'

Sam laughed. 'Bigarse, paid me well but I didn't like him. Look – I've done business with millionaires and billionaires and they've been nice guys, but Bigarse was arrogant. I'm a professional ship architect but he treated me like a grubby oik.'

'And the wife?'

'Didn't really know her, But she seemed a nice little thing. Too good for Bigarse, but then with his money he could have any woman.'

Dave thought for a moment. 'Did Blake-Grass have enemies?'

'Almost certainly I would guess. But it was the wife that did for him wasn't it?'

'The police are questioning her but I think the case against her is doubtful.'

Sam frowned. 'I would still question that bloke Ternby. He was supposed to be aboard the ship that night.' He pointed to his computer. 'I've a commission in hand for Magnum Millennium, but Bigarse was the principal shareholder and I don't know what'll happen to the company now.'

'Most likely be bought by a Russian or an Arab prince.'

'I've just seen the local news on TV,' said Emily. 'The police have asked for more time to question Cerise Blake-Grass about her husband's murder.'

'I dunno',' replied Tom. 'Did she really do it or are the law stuck for a result?'

'We may never know until she comes for trial.'

'Will Travis be prosecuting her?'

'Possibly, but they wouldn't let me do it. It's got to be someone neutral.'

'Your Dad said that Cerise knew something about the Jebbs killing.'

'Yes,' said Emily. 'But she never said what. By the way, I had a call on my mobile from Josie. She's going house hunting in the Winchester area and I've invited her and Dave to dinner tonight.'

'If she's expecting they'll need a bigger place than that flat they're in.'

'Lorraine told me she's going to sell their house in Old Alresford,' said Emily.

'That's sad. I went there once and it's a nice little house on the edge of town – would suit them fine.'

'Lorraine's given me their front door key. She asked me to fetch some things for her. She doesn't want to go back herself: too many memories.'

'All right,' said Tom. 'I've got time off this afternoon we could do the job then.'

'It's her account books and one or two things like that. She owes money and although she's getting some sort of widow's pension she doesn't know how much yet. I'm going to talk to Tony Travis and see where she stands with government compensation.'

'Quite right too. Poor Wally died doing his duty.'

'Where are we looking for?' asked Tom. They had reached the little town of Alresford only minutes from their home.

'You'll have to turn right into Broad Street,' said Emily. 'The house is in Old Alresford near the cricket ground.'

'Of course. I was only there once and that was after dark and you driving.'

'Just as well I was driving. You'd been on the booze.'

Emily liked Alresford; a delightful small town with an almost chocolate-box aura. For the time being there were no huge out of town supermarkets but many small specialist shops. Emily had never regretted moving to within a couple of miles of this delightful place.

She guided Tom to Old Alresford and found the empty Markham

house. 'Let's hope no thieves have turned the place over,' she said. 'That would be the final straw.'

They reached the house: in fact a little redbrick bungalow, detached and with a neat garden. Emily and Tom left the warmth of the car and stood in the road feeling the rush of freezing air surround them. 'Let's get inside,' said Tom.

The house was almost as cold as the outside winter. Emily didn't know where the heating system was and anyway it would seem wrong to switch it on. 'I'll go into Wally's computer cubby hole,' she said. 'Lorraine's asked for her bathrobe and her bedroom telly. Could you go and find them?'

'I have my orders,' he laughed and crossed the hallway to the main bedroom.

Emily examined Wally's desk. This was much harder than she had expected. She felt tears in her eyes and a lump in her throat as she pulled open drawers and checked the little filing cabinet. She knew Wally was a tidy individual and she found the papers and household account books with no problem. The light on the telephone answer was flashing. Emily thought about it and then pressed the button. Two no-number call centres and one about a parcel delivery. Then:

"Mr Markham, I wouldn't go with that prisoner from Lewes jail if I was you. He's bad news. That's a warning…' Then the message cut short. Emily acted now. She ripped both telephone and answer unit from their sockets and crammed them into an empty bin liner beside Wally's desk.

'Tom' she called. 'We'll have to take this to the police and right now.'

CHAPTER 14

Inspector Marchway had been summoned by his chief. The two had worked together for many years and both well remembered the last Hamble murder and the others that followed. They had suffered the ignominy of solving the case via information from that journalist Manning. Now the tiresome Manning and the Daily Banner were already sniffing around this investigation.

Chief Superintendent Hollins waved Marchway to a chair. 'Garry,' he said. 'We've a problem. Crown prosecution are not satisfied with the case you've brought against Mrs Blake-Grass.'

'Sir, why? She was there when it happened and she held the murder weapon: her prints are on it.'

'I know, the heavy pipe wrench. But it was a plumbing tool, not part of the yacht's kit and she only held it very daintily with the finger tips before she dropped it. Forensics are definite about that. No other prints on it.'

'I've only got two hours of questioning left, sir.'

'You'll have to release her on bail. Also we've been told there was a man who was supposed to be aboard that night. He's Darren Ternby the ship's engineer.'

'But he's made a statement already. He came back to the yacht and saw the Blake-Grass wife standing on the yacht's stern wailing and screaming.'

Hollins shook his head. 'That's hardly surprising and not the actions of a cold-blooded killer. I don't want to intrude in your investigation, but I suggest you take a closer look at this man, Ternby.'

'All right, I'll release the Blake-Grass woman, but she'll be under restriction.'

'Right, we've another development in the Jebbs affair. Sussex have sent me this. It was handed in to us but we passed it on as it's their investigation.' Hollins held up a CD in a transparent case. 'This is a tape of an answerphone message found in Wallace Markham's house. It warns Markham not to go on the prison van that day. You'll find that the voice is most respectful; calls him "Mister Markham".'

'Oh, yes,' Marchway was interested. 'Respectful and Mister – that sounds like an ex- jail inmate. Markham was a warder but they liked him.'

'We're co-operating with Sussex on the Jebbs business.'

'I know, sir. It's not just Markham – there's that man Jones. He was as bent as a paper clip.'

Hollins laughed. 'That's a most apt analogy.'

Cerise was in a mind-blanked state. She felt detached from the world: a zombie.

'Mrs Blake-Grass, did you understand me?' The interrogator was staring at her.

She nodded; speech was beyond her. 'You are released on police bail. You will not be allowed to return to your home address but you must register a new address where you are compelled to live and not to leave without permission.'

Cerise nodded again.

'Very well, please give us the details to our entry desk.' The awful man waved a dismissal.

'Come on, dear,' whispered the woman PC. 'You can fill up the form out here.'

Away from the interrogator Cerise found her voice. 'I want to ring my sister. I'd like to stay with her. I don't want to go to my own house anyway.'

'That's all right. Just let's fill in the forms and you can sign them.' At least this woman was kindly. Maybe she didn't believe that Cerise was guilty.

With help she completed the forms and signed them.

'We've a car to run you to your sister's house,' said the PC.

They arrived at the East Meon house and Cerise thanked the driver. Her sister, Jasmine raced out of the front to door and hugged her.

'Please, Jazz. Have you told Ifor I'm going to be here?'

'Yes, I rang him as soon as I heard. He was a bit grumpy but he's OK about it.'

'Thank God for that. Oh, Jazz, I wish I knew why he's so down on me.'

'Oh, Ifor's all right really. He's a bit suspicious of the normal world. He's Welsh and a bit of a puritan.'

Gradually Cerise returned to the normal world. She missed Graham, really mourned for him and she would never get over the horror of his dead body. That dominated everything and even blanked out the misery of her interrogation by that stupid copper.

She was glad to be with her older sister and she would do everything to get in the good books of Ifor.

Ifor had arrived home at seven o'clock that evening. He threw off his overcoat and poured himself a whisky and a slug of gin for each of the girls. Cerise was watchful, but Ifor's attitude had definitely softened. 'I'm sorry about poor old Graham,' he said. 'But I know you wouldn't touch him. I'd be looking at that Ternby. Surly brute, in my experience.'

Cerise sipped her drink. The alcohol was soothing but it didn't suppress her grief. 'We knew Darren, he fixed the boat's engines, but he got on fine with Graham and he was well paid for it. No, Ifor, someone hated Graham and I want that person caught. I'll never be free of this until that happens.'

Darren Ternby had gone to the police in Southampton of his own volition. Of course he was nervous but everything in past experience told him that it was better to steal a march as it were and not to wait for the cops to find him. Of course he should have been aboard the yacht and not out with his girl but, there was no person left to fire him from his job and the yacht's future was uncertain. The police interview had been a complete anticlimax, The interviewing copper had waved away Darren's made up excuse for not being on the yacht, but had asked a long list of questions about Cerise and her behaviour. He was relieved, at least the cops didn't suspect him and anyway, his girl and the barman at the pub had already agreed to support him. It seemed they were determined to pin the killing on Cerise and he was uncertain about that. He hadn't told the police about the man he'd seen crouched by the dockside crane. He knew he should have, but the man was so well known he doubted the law would believe him. At least he had been reassured that he would still be paid although it seemed unlikely that *Conqueror* would be going anywhere soon. He was only an engineer but he couldn't forget that dodgy South American voyage. He'd been drawn into something very nasty that time as an innocent witness,

Darren left the police station and drove home to his lodging in Eastleigh. Once there he would pour himself a stiff whisky and take a nap. His girl, Carrie, was working and wouldn't be home for an hour. He was annoyed to find that his flat door was unlocked. Hell, it wasn't as if he had that much to steal. Angrily he flung open the door and stormed inside. He barely felt the iron bar that crushed his skull.

53

CHAPTER 15

Lorraine's house had yet to go on the market and she had asked that Dave and Josie should consider it first. They had travelled to Old Alresford with Emily and Tom, not sure what to expect.

'Nice double garage,' remarked Dave. 'Room for a car and boat in there.'

'Oh yeah,' said Emily. 'Whose car is the one that sits out in winter? Josie's I guess.'

They went indoors and poked around the little bungalow and, for the first time, climbed the narrow stairs to the little chalet style room in the roof. Emily left Dave and Josie and went down to join Tom who was making coffee. He had turned on the little TV set in a corner of the kitchen. The local news was showing.

'All gloom and doom,' said Tom. 'It's all road closures, and some guy's been beaten to death in a house breaking in Eastleigh, and Pompey Football Club are broke.'

'My Dad supports Southampton. He played for their youth team. And it looks as if it's going to snow,' said Emily glancing out of the window.

'I don't see the connection,' Tom laughed. 'Anyway I'm a Dorset man. Your local feuds don't apply to me.'

Emily went out and called upstairs. 'Coffee's up, you two.'

'Dave and Josie appeared. 'I've turned on the heating,' said Emily. 'Lorraine wants it on anyway in case of damp.'

'Warmest place is in here,' said Tom pointing to the tiny sitting room.

'What did the police say about the answerphone?' asked Dave. 'My editor says they can't touch it as a story until the police make a statement.'

'Just as I said,' Tom replied. 'They just took the message and of course, no comment.'

Dave was rummaging in a filing tray filled with letters. 'Should you be doing that?' asked Josie.

'I'm a journalist and – oh my God. This is amazing!'

'What've you found?' asked Tom.

'Well this letter comes from an address in Somerset and it's signed by Amanda Furness. She's the school teacher that Jebbs killed and my

54

editor says she was what the tabloids call a love child.'

'So what,' said Emily. 'If this great big yob hadn't married me, poor little Peter would have been one too.'

'No, no! That's not the point. My editor had done some digging and he says the teacher's father was Graham Blake-Grass.'

'I wonder,' said Emily. 'I wonder if Cerise knew that?'

'Amanda was Jebbs' ex-wife, said Tom. 'Even if Cerise put him up to it, there was no call for Jebbs to kill those people. They were local and some of them middle aged. They couldn't all have been sired by Bigarse.'

Emily glared. 'There's no need to be so callous. It was a massacre of innocents.'

'I'll have to show the letter to Lorraine,' said Dave. 'Then I'll scan a copy before I give it to the police.'

'What's it about?' asked Emily.

'Read it yourself,' said Dave. 'But to summarise it says that she knows that Jones was supplying kids to paedophiles.'

'Why tell Loraine? Except, this Amanda; she must have known that Wally knew Jones.'

'Another warning?' said Tom.

'Seems likely.'

Now his world had gone crazy and Inspector Marchway was in a foul mood. A vital witness was dead – murdered. Darren Ternby, the man who had seen Cerise Blake-Grass with her husband's murdered body. That murder had taken place a little after midday and Cerise was definitely at her sister's house during that time. Now he would have to report to his chief that they had reached a dead end. No suspects, no leads and five sensational murders that would bring the news media screaming down on his head.

A young WPC was hovering trying to catch his eye. He guessed she knew what sort of mood he was in and expected an explosion. 'Please, sir, please.'

'Yes, what is it?'

'We've got a Ms Carrie McArdle in the interview room. She says she's Mr Ternby's friend and she says he told her something that you should know.'

Marchway found the girl looking tearful and nervous as he would expect. 'Hello, Ms McArdle. Can I help you?' Marchway forced himself to be soothing.

She broke down in tears. 'He's gone and I don't believe it. Please will you catch who did it?'

'We're working on it right now. Whoever did this will pay for it. I promise.'

The girl looked up at him her face was wet with tears. 'Darren told me yesterday. He said he should have told you but he didn't want to get involved. But just after the murder of that Bigarse guy on the yacht Darren saw another man he knew on the dockside and the man turned and hid his face.'

Marchway was interested now. 'Did he give you a name.'

'Sorry, but he said he didn't want to be involved, but he was surprised to see this person there.'

Marchway forced himself to be patient. 'It's a name we need and then we can involve this man or eliminate him.'

'All Darren said was that he knew the man and that this bloke knew that bastard Jones.'

CHAPTER 16

That night the threatened snow came and with it gusts of wind that filled the roads and blocked the lane leading to Emily and Tom's house.

'The mainline phone's still working,' said Emily. 'I've only got one minor court case but I guess the snow may have called off all hearings today.'

'Not so good for me,' grumbled Tom as he stared out of the window. 'I'm supposed to be in Weston-Super-Mare at three p.m.'

'Sunny seaside in January,' laughed Emily. 'You'd better ring and cancel.'

'I suppose so, but it won't gain me any favours with my boss man.'

'Oh, come on. You've done six days a week for years, apart from the weddings and our time in Olifa. This is a nationwide emergency. Nobody can accuse you of skiving.'

Tom still looked gloomy. 'I suppose the council will open the main road, but nobody's coming up here until the farmer gets going with his tractor and front loader.'

'Can't see the postman getting here either. However I got my most important item two days ago.' Emily held up the still wrapped pregnancy testing kit.

'You can't use that yet surely – too early.'

'No but in another week I will.'

Cerise woke up to the news of this further death. Darren Ternby had been the man who ran the engine room on *Conqueror* and sometimes in port he doubled as a security guard.

He was a strong built fellow and nice mannered, if rather quiet. Now the horror bit home. Was this connected with Graham's death? Ternby was supposed to be watching the ship that night. She hadn't seen him aboard but he must have been on patrol on the dock. She gasped as the thought came to her. Had Ternby killed Graham and done it while she slept below decks? But why should he have done that? Graham had been good to him, he'd trusted him. She grieved for her lost husband as she had never grieved before, but there had always been dark side to him. Graham was a very powerful man in his own world and he orchestrated things that were not always within the law. And he knew

57

something. He knew in advance about that awful slaughter over in Sussex. She had overheard him talking to a visitor in their house. It had been a covert conversation about Jebbs and mention had been made of someone called Jones. "No loss, time for him to go…"

She had assumed this was some business deal; maybe a deal that was not quite straight in the eyes of the taxman. She hadn't cared to ask Graham about it. He would have been angry; telling her to keep her nose out. Her duty was to be the good little wife and entertain guests and business associates with foods and wine and the master himself later in bed. She knew she should have resented this but Graham was her life and now he was gone she felt lost.

At least Ifor had softened his attitude. She could never understand Jasmine's fascination for this man. Ifor was wealthy and successful, but with the current austerity boats were not everyone's first priority. She and Jasmine were London girls as had been Graham, but Ifor was a Welshman and a Welsh speaking Welshman to the point where he proudly boasted that English was his second language. Yesterday he and Jasmine had gone twice to Southampton to a church called the Cymraeg Forgather. Jasmine had become quite hooked by the singing and had learned a limited version of the language. She was much less enamoured, she said, by the minister who gave his address in English. The homily was mostly about sin, and sin included: rock music, alcohol and seemingly frowned on educating girls. The man's sermons could have doubled without comment in a mosque. Ifor ignored the condemnation of alcohol and music, but Jasmine had had to fight him hard to let their daughter, Meredydd go to university. This was partly religious ideology but mostly that Ifor had reserved a place for Meredydd in his office.

Cerise was under police restriction, ordered not to leave this house or its surroundings.

Now that the snows had fallen, blocking roads for miles, the restrictions seemed a bit daft. She was determined to stay calm and hope that the police would have enough sense to look for the real murderer. That at least would bring some sort of temporary closure, but she still mourned for Graham and always would.

London was cold and some of the pavements were still icy. But the tube system was operating as normal. Dave left the Bayswater flat and took the line to the Banner offices on Canary Wharf. He found the crime editor in his office, and then tried his best to convince the man that Hampshire was off limits with snowbound roads and that even the motorways were only partly navigable.

'Not to worry, we've found a trail to Jebbs right here in the smoke,' the crime editor was staring at his computer screen. 'Dear old Sid gave us a tip off on Tuesday.'

Dave was startled. 'What, Sid Everett, doesn't he ever give up?'

The editor laughed. 'No, retirement doesn't suit him. The police haven't caught on that Jebbs had a little studio right here, not a mile from where we're sitting. Sid wangled the door key from somewhere and he's had a good look.'

The editor clicked his mouse and a video shone on the computer screen. 'Come and have a sight at this saucy stuff. Better than shooting boats.'

'Good God,' Dave gasped. The two naked persons, male and female, seemed to going at it with gusto. Nothing staged, but the man was all too familiar.

CHAPTER 17

'We think this was a sneaky Pete video,' said the editor.

'A what?'

'Oh, David, you are the soul of innocence. Are all you Kiwis so pure?'

'I've no idea. Please explain.'

'We guess that Jebbs made this video without the knowledge of the actors. Sid checked the files in the studio. This video dates back a year or so, but Jebbs wrote a reference. It looks as if it was shot in the Southampton area and the market for the film was South America.'

'But nobody can be charged for anything,' said Dave.

'But there could be several vengeful persons wanting Jebbs disposed of before his trial. No knowing what might have come out then.'

'Have you shown this to the police?'

'Not yet, they'd probably do Sid for breaking and entering.'

'Not for the first time,' said Dave.

'Farmer says he'll clear the lane midday tomorrow,' said Tom. 'No good before that, because the wind'll likely fill it all in again.'

Emily laughed. 'Well, we can have a cosy day off – just the three of us and hopefully the one inside me.'

'You seem mighty sure of that.'

'Well, don't fret; if so it'll be another eight months and there's nothing to stop us having fun well before that happens.'

'Then there's the long gap with no fun as you put it.' Tom sounded gloomy.

Emily became serious. 'We haven't heard a thing from Dave.'

'I guess he's stuck in London. His investigation will be dead for a while and so I guess will the official one. Nobody's going far in this weather.'

Emily smiled now. 'If only Peter was a little bit older we could make him a snowman.'

Tom grinned. 'Let's build one anyway.'

Emily put her arms around him. 'Oh yes, let's. Husband, I love you.'

'And I love you, and always will.'

Dave hurried home to Bayswater. The flat was deliciously warm although God only knew what that was costing. Josie was working at her computer. 'Nearly finished this one, then it's off to the editor. She'll have some nitpicks, she always does but then it's the proof reader and another book launch.'

Dave kissed her on her forehead. 'How are things: anymore tummy trouble?'

'Morning sickness, but it doesn't necessarily come in the morning. I hope I'm past that stage. So, you can take me out and buy me a gourmet Italian meal.'

'That's sounds more like it. Reckon you can walk to la Pizzareta? It's bloody cold out there?'

'As long as I put sensible walking shoes on I'll be fine. Tell me, how was your visit to the scurrilous Banner?'

'I had a shock and then some. It looks definite that the solution to these murders is down in Hampshire and, weird as it may seem, it's getting mired in the Ollavasen case again.'

'But the murderer was caught and put away. We were there.'

'Yes, and I'll always remember it. But there's a figure from that time who is somehow involved, and until I've uninvolved him I'm not letting go.'

'You mean someone involved in sailing.'

'Sailing, yes and you could say yachting with a capital Y.'

'Oh, come on who is it?'

He told her the whole story and she gasped.

Dave was never going to be spooked by bad weather. Snowfall and delayed journeys were not entirely novel. In childhood he had spent time with his uncle and aunt in the South Island. In winter it had snowed and then some. In those days his uncle had driven around the farm in an old American half-track vehicle, a relic of World War Two and the jungles of New Guinea. Wisely, Dave had left the car in London and taken the train for Southampton. It was frustrating with two changes and long delays but he got there and put up for the night in a hotel; at the Banner's expense of course.

He was not going to blunder straight into the suspect's office and announce who he was. By now the man would know that Dave was a journalist and probably engaged in phone hacking and all things dubious. It was after midday and he was feeling hungry. A pub offered refuge from the freezing street and the menu board looked inviting. He went in and there was his first piece of luck that day. By the bar stood a man he knew.

'Hi Ed, how you doing?'

Ed Coulden, the offshore yachtsman had briefly been a suspect in the Ollavasen murder.

Ed had a puzzled look then he grinned. 'Kiwi Dave the journo, I didn't recognise you in that woolly cap.'

'That's because it's bloody cold. Back home it's midsummer.'

Ed laughed. 'Well, it's like Midsomer Murders here. That's why you're sniffing around I guess.'

'Oh, come on. I'm a sports writer, but I must say everything I've heard points the finger at these parts.'

'In that you are dead right and it's got me scared. A lot of posh people know a lot about it and they're not saying.'

'Come on, Ed, I'll buy you a drink. Have you eaten yet? Well, come on I'll do the honours and it's all on my expenses.'

'So you are nosing around.'

'My paper want me to listen, but only if these crimes have a connection with sailing.'

'Well, you could say that.'

They found a table and Dave plied his guest with beer and a full blown steak and chips meal. Ed was a fully qualified yachtmaster who had skippered charter yachts in the Mediterranean. These yachts were run by Mulberry Charters in nearby Hamble and the boss of this outfit was one of the men whom Dave was concerned with.

'Yeah,' said Ed. 'That shit Jebbs took some shots of boats all around Hamble. Good thing he's gone, although he should've been hanged in a jail and not by that mad crew.'

'Who would you say were the mad crew, or if you like, who planned it?'

'I'd say Bigarse. He always thought he was beyond the law. He had money in all the firms around these parts, anything to do with boats.'

'I know that. Steve Simpson said he was a big shareholder in his sailmaking company.'

'No, no,' said Ed. 'Simpson's a good straight guy, but just about the only one.'

'Tell me about the ones who are not quite so straight? And why should Blake-Grass have been mixed up in all this?'

'Bigarse, we all called him. We reckon Jebbs was screwing one of his women, maybe that was the one he killed.'

'No, Ed, Amanda Furness was Jebbs' ex-wife, Furness is her second husband's surname, but she was also Bigarse's daughter but not by any wife.'

'Yeah, that follows; bet she wasn't the only one.'

'Tell me who Bigarse had some hold over?'

'Well Jebbs for a start...'

'Yes, but he's dead.'

'All right, the living. My old boss for one.'

'Who are we talking about?'

'Richard Halderholm,'

David remembered the chief of Mulberry Charters. Halderholm was a successful business man who had a record of a violent temper.

'You worked for him.'

'Not any more. Got a better job now, I work for Sam Pollingham. Much better job in winter.'

'You design yachts?' Dave was surprised. From what he'd recently found out, Sam Pollingham might know a few of the answers.

'No, but Sam runs a brokerage and I sell boats for him. Sell all types and sizes. It's a good job – suits me and it pays well.'

Dave thought carefully. 'Jebbs is dead but did you know the two men who were murdered with him?'

'I saw Markham around the scene but he was a dinghy man. He was the one married to a darkie. They seemed a nice couple.'

'What about the other prison warder, Jones?'

'I don't like to think about him – bastard.'

Dave changed tack. 'What can you tell me about Jebbs?'

Ed to a swig of beer and stared mournfully at his empty glass. Dave went to the bar for a replacement. 'Now Jebbs, please; everything you know.'

Ed gave a humourless laugh. 'Drove around in a swanky car. Did well for himself and he never got that from snapping boats.'

'So, where did this wealth come from?'

'He made and sold porno films and that dodgy bloke from Olifa marketed them in South America.'

'Do you mean Garcia?'

'Yup, good yacht helm in his day, but after what he tried to do to little Emily and the other girls was evil. Got his comeuppance then all right.'

Dave felt a rare sense of triumph. His breakthrough was confirmed with Garcia in the frame. Garcia was back on the superrich list, but there had been several months when he was holed up not far away in Hampshire. So Jebbs' dubious art work must have been a financial lifeline.

'Did Garcia ever take part in the action? I mean did he act in any of the films?'

'Shouldn't think so. He put up the money and shared the loot with Jebbs.'

'Ed, how do you know all this?'

Ed roared with embarrassed laughter. 'If you must know I was one of his actors. Me and my girl did it on the deck of a yacht in the sunshine. Got paid good money for the fun.'

Dave was startled. 'Not in the main channel at Hamble?'

'No, we were anchored just off the nudie beach at Studland. But of course we didn't make it too obvious. Nobody noticed.'

'What you're telling me is that there could be any number of actors, as you phrase it who would be happy to see Jebbs out of the way.'

'You'll be dead right there.'

Dave drank his own beer. 'Dead is the key word I'd say.'

CHAPTER 18

'Sir, we've found the police car they used in the road block.'

Chief Constable Fox, of Sussex Constabulary, looked up from his desk to see an excited Detective Sergeant.

'Well done,' he replied. 'It is definitely the right one?'

'Oh yes, sir. It was hidden up a woodland track only a hundred metres from the scene. I don't know why it fooled the prison van driver. It's an old model and it's not even one of ours. It comes from Tyneside in the nineteen eighties. We've checked.'

'Geordie land, eh? What have they got to say about it?'

'We're checking with them now, sir.'

The sergeant left the room and Fox mused. This multi murder had all the stamp of a military operation: precision timing and planning. The Hampshire force had contacted him with news of two further murders with assumed connection to Jebbs and the others. Blake-Grass the multi-billionaire might have had a reason to kill Jebbs and the resources to plan it. His wife had been released on bail, but frankly she sounded an unlikely killer. From London the Met had had a tip off about a studio that Jebbs had used in the city. It was set up to make porno videos. Somewhere amongst all this was a solution, but his team of twenty officers working flat out had achieved nothing. Not their fault. They were up against some sophisticated criminals.

Frankly, only two months away from retirement, he could do without all this. Once again there would have to be a press conference and a confrontation with the news pack and the TV media. The snow blizzard had only half abated and Fox had had a struggle to drive to work from his family home in Bosham. He certainly admired the tenacity of his officers in finding that car in this weather. He would make a point of saying so to the press.

The farmer had cleared the lane to their house and the overnight temperature drop had stabilised the snow banks on either side. Lily had slid up the lane in her little car and would be looking after Peter and the house for the day. Emily was prosecuting two minor cases in Winchester, and Tom was finally on his way to the West Country. On this occasion he would have company. Dave Manning had rung them from a hotel in Southampton and had dropped it that he needed to get to Somerset. Tom had business in Weston-Super-Mare and Dave was following his story to some place near there. They surmised, correctly, that Dave was following a lead in the Jebbs murder or, more important to them, the ruthless killing of their friend, Wally.

Dave had been considerate and had taken a taxi to Alresford, an expense presumably met by the Daily Banner. 'I'm in luck,' he said. 'Jebbs committed his atrocity in a village called Little Hollingberry and Josie's stepfather and her mother live seven miles away. And don't worry, Tom. The Banner have fixed me a hire car in Weston and after that it's not far to go.'

Tom realised only too well that Dave had to be circumspect. He couldn't charge in with foot in the door to a scene of such grief. Dave was the right man to follow this trail whereas a journalist like the infamous Sid Everett would be a disaster. In the end the road trip could have been worse. The motorways and main A-roads were clear and salted and gritted. Fortunately Tom's car heater was in good fettle, and that eased the journey. They made one stop for a meal and to refuel. The cost at the pumps was extortionate but although Dave offered to share the cost, Tom declined saying his company would pick up the bill this time. It was dark when they arrived in the Somerset seaside resort on the coast of the Bristol Channel. Sunny and happy in summer, the town was bleak and sad in January. Tom found his hotel and Dave was not too late to pick up his hire car. The hire firm office manager grumbled a bit at mention of the Daily Banner and looked at Dave suspiciously.

Dave took the road heading north towards Bristol. He had visited Josie's parents' house once before when they had sailed a regatta on the nearby Chew reservoir, now a sheet of ice. He reached the house and was welcomed with real warmth by Janet and her husband, Lance. Lance was a local doctor, settled happily in Somerset although he was an American born and bred in New Jersey.

Janet flung her arms around Dave and Lance shook his hand warmly. 'Say I wish we'd stayed in your Kiwi land a bit longer after the wedding.'

Dave agreed. 'Josie and me wanted to stay on but my paper recalled me.'

Lance and Janet glanced at each other. 'Yes, we understand they want you to report on these horrible things that happened.'

'Yes, that's about it, but it's the sailing connection and that's my scene.'

Janet spoke quietly. 'We'll help if we can and we think we may be able to.'

Cerise was scared now. The police had summoned her to return to the central police station for another interrogation. Jasmine had offered to drive her there and wait until the interview was over. But would she be coming back again? Cerise could not stand the thought of another couple of nights in police custody; she would sooner die. If she died would she be joining Graham? Ifor would probably say that would be in hell, but what had she ever done to be punished in hell? What had she done anyway and why couldn't that thick copper see that she had loved Graham and couldn't have killed him.

Jasmine's powerful Audi was not the ideal car for the icy roads around East Meon and it was a relief to reach the broad M27. In next to no time they were parking by the police headquarters. Jasmine gave her sister a supportive hug and then they both entered the warm reception area.

'Mrs Blake-Grass,' the inspector began. 'We have some reassuring news. As from today you are no longer subject to restriction but we would ask you to be available should we feel you could help us.'

Cerise was tearful in her relief. 'Will you catch who did it?'

'Dear lady, we will do that. I am confident.'

Cerise was asked or compelled to sign a whole lot of confusing paperwork and then they were once more out in the freezing air of the car park.

'Let's get you home,' Said Jasmine. She swore. 'What the bloody hell was the point of us driving all this way just for that? He could have phoned us.'

CHAPTER 19

'We've been haunted by that horrible carnage for months,' said Janet. 'Mrs Furness was a popular teacher and two of the people slaughtered were big names in this community.' Her voice broke. 'Oh, that is what terrifies everyone around here.'

'And why did that madman pick on those particular people?' said Lance. 'They had nothing to do with him.'

Dave was puzzled. 'I know nothing about this, and my paper hasn't much idea who they were. There was nothing about grieving spouses and children and the Banner would have revelled in that.'

'Yes,' said Lance. 'There you have it...'

Janet intervened. 'They were all local people apart from that Hopeson woman.'

'Please can you tell me more?'

'Well, we didn't like her, Gloria Hopeson. She was a local business woman. She was also the prospective Conservative candidate for this area. The current MP is a Lib Dem and they were hoping this Hopeson would oust him.'

'Do you know what business this Hopeson lady was engaged in and did she have a husband?'

'She had just divorced and the ex-husband was granted part care of their only daughter. He was involved in the business she ran and she somehow unloaded him from that. He had a bigger grievance than this mad Jebbs. Her business was, and in fact still is, something to do with long distance haulage.'

Yes, thought Dave. Now he had a connection. But why should Jebbs have killed her or any of the others? That was the question that everyone had asked. There was theory enough about Jebbs' mental state, but no evidence to support that he was a deranged mass-killer. Now was the moment to tell them his real interest.

'As you know two prison officers died. The man Jones was corrupt, but Wallace Markham was a friend of me and Josie. We sailed together. I've been asked to follow the connections with boats and sailing.'

Janet looked grim. 'We know; Josie told us when she phoned. She says that Markham's wife works in a hospital and she was midwife to a friend of yours.'

'That's right. It was Emily Stoneman's baby. Emily and Tom are friends of ours. We all sail, but Emily is famous, she won Olympic gold.'

'Oh, yes,' now Lance smiled. 'We remember them from your wedding. And young Emily; she was one of the three girls that beat our US girls in the final race. We saw it on TV – kinda' exciting, though I don't know sailing.'

Dave wondered if he should try further. 'Please, there is evidence that the man Jones was putting perverts in touch with kids from a children's home and the evidence is that home was near Bristol.'

'Yeah,' said Lance. 'Seems, that guy was a real jerk.'

Janet was angry. 'We've heard this, but why in hell didn't the police do something?'

'Did anyone encounter Jebbs before the murders?'

'No,' replied Janet. 'We'd never heard of him but it seems he was Amanda's ex-husband or so the press say. But she ditched him and she married again.'

'Her widowed husband works in Bristol. He lectures at the university,' said Lance.

'Yes,' said Janet. 'Nice bloke by all accounts. They say he's a Yorkshireman though.'

Dave grinned. 'This UK north-south thing. We've got a bit of that where I come from but with us it's two separate islands. Auckland, where we were married, is very cosmopolitan, but we tend to laugh at the Southern Islanders, although my old mum's a southerner.'

'We really liked what we saw of your country,' said Lance. 'That big girl Chloe was quite a character.'

'She was Emily's gold medal skipper, but Chloe's a sort of aristocrat. She's a Maori; descended from a long line of chiefs.' Dave needed to take his questions forward. 'One thing we know about Jebbs is that he was a sports photographer, but his big earner was porno films.'

Lance laughed. 'Not my style. Gave up on those years ago after college.'

'Oh, really,' said Janet. 'What about all those naked girls in your desk drawer?'

'Sounds a bit of a tight fit,' laughed Dave.

'Don't take any notice,' replied Lance. 'We to them away from Josie's little brother.'

In Hampshire, Superintendent Hollins was even more baffled. He no longer needed an arranged cooperation with the Sussex force. The powers that be had now declared both forces united in a single investigation. It was simply that he was puzzled by the report that had arrived on his desk. Along with the prison service, his force and several others had pooled detailed research on the character of the killer Jebbs. The man seemed to have been not only mad but to be a total contradiction. Jebbs had made a living as a sports photographer but to enhance his income he made porn videos. These he marketed overseas. How did that square with reliable reports that Jebbs was obsessively religious? That had been one of the alleged reasons why his school teacher wife had thrown him out of their house and divorced him. Surely one so intensely religious should not murder an unfaithful wife, and should not all life be sacrosanct? No, there was something wrong here and he wasn't sure he had the stamina to get to the bottom of the mystery. Tracing the Blake-Grass killer or killers was now his primary task. Whether the other dead man, Ternby, had been connected with this was a possibility but that crime was still officially a house breaking that had gone sour. Sussex had found the counterfeit police car but there had been no trace of the white transit van. Hardly surprising that when one vehicle in five was some sort of white van. He had been forced to accept that he had extracted all the information he could from the Blake-Grass wife. He wished he could interrogate that tiresome journalist, Manning. The man had been sniffing round the sailing scene for his own selfish ends and had seemingly vanished or, more likely, he was holed up in London with this bad weather. Well, Hollins was not going to ring the Daily Banner to find the man. Now he craved a cigarette but that would mean going out into the freezing cold car park. He sighed, stood up and went to the canteen for some breakfast.

Emily was excited and pleased. She felt a warm glow of success and couldn't wait to tell her husband. Two things had pleased her, with one overwhelmingly important. She had had a compliment from a judge for her handling of a defence. Not in open court but in a confidential message passed to her. That was good but far more important was the fact that her pregnancy test had proved positive. They were going to have a little sibling for Peter.

Tom had left forty eight hours ago for the West Country taking Dave with him. Tom had computer systems to work on for his firm, but Dave was following a trail in this horrible mass murder. So far she hadn't had a call from either of them. So both Josie and she were expecting although Josie's child was due first in four months in fact. Lily would arrive in a few minutes to help with Peter. The roads were much better and the lane had now been gritted. She looked out of the window and saw Lily's car and behind it a second one that looked familiar. That was odd and unexpected; the second car was Josie's and Emily could see her behind the wheel. What on earth? She thought Josie was in London while Dave was away. Well she had news for Josie and they could talk babies.

But Josie was not in a mood to talk babies. She was white faced and clearly frightened. 'Oh Em, I'm scared. I've tried to ring Dave but he's not picking up his mobile. I rang home but Mum says he's left for Bristol.'

Emily was concerned. Her friend was clearly very frightened. 'Please Josie, what's happened?'

'A man rang our flat and he said Dave would come to harm if he didn't stop asking about Jebbs.'

CHAPTER 20

Josie had spent a quiet day in the flat, only defying the cold outside to walk as far as the Co-op supermarket. Following the horrors of last year, plus loyalty to her friend Donna, she didn't care to use the nearer branch of Qualistores. She was beginning to feel the child inside her womb. Though the fact made her so happy, it did slow her down. Only four months to go and they would be a family of three. She staggered home with ten days supply of food and other essentials and this time to the lift rather than climb the stairs. The flat was warm, and a nice chat show was on the telly. She wondered how Dave was getting on. She supposed she could trust him to be circumspect in his questioning and not offend people. Dave had once worked with the infamous Sid Everett but he would never use Everett's intrusion. Dave had stayed overnight in her Mum and Lance's house and had then said he was going to Bristol.

Then the phone rang. Oh good, this should be Dave, she wasn't expecting any other calls. No, instead a disembodied robotic voice.

'Mrs Manning, listen with care. Stop your husband from asking questions that he has no business to ask. Tell him to come home and stick to little boats…' The voice cut abruptly.

Josie rang Dave's mobile again and again and still the tiresome man didn't pick up. She rang her Mum's home again but only heard an answerphone voice. What the hell was Dave doing in Bristol? She knew the city well, and had gained her degree at the university. She gave up, grabbed a few things into her overnight bag and fled.

Dave found the newspaper offices. He was pointed to a waiting room which was at least warm compared with the icy north wind outside. He had an appointment with a sports editor he knew. He wasn't sure how helpful the man would be but Dave was prepared to be frank and hoped the man's natural journalist's curiosity would be brought into play.

It took half an hour before an obese woman summoned Dave and waved him into a lift.

'Mr Ormerod will see you. First floor, third door on the right.'

Dave found the door and knocked. This time a rather pretty PA smiled and pointed him inside to where Dave's friend Simon Ormerod was seated at his computer screen.

'Not much weather for sailing today,' Simon greeted him. 'Chew lake is frozen and there's even reports of the sea freezing; not round here – tide's too fast.'

Dave knew Simon who also sailed. Although sports-wise the man was devoted to Bristol City FC and Bath Rugby club. Dave was ambivalent about football but as a New Zealander he loved rugby. He had got to know Simon and they had watched games together the previous year.

'Tea or coffee?' whispered the girl PA.

'Hot coffee would be brilliant,' Dave smiled in return.

The coffee arrived and the PA tactfully retreated into another room.

'All right, big Dave,' Simon grinned. 'You can't fool me we've had news of your investigations. So I'm prepared. I can send you down to our crime man but I doubt he knows much more than I can tell you.'

Dave gaped. 'How do you know what I'm after?'

'Well, it's a very small world and it seems the South Coast cops have told our local cops that you're on the Jebbs case and I guess they think people will talk to you when they'll only clam up with the police. Am I right?'

Dave worried. He must be horribly naïve to think he could keep his mission concealed. The world of journalism was a small one. 'I don't know about all that,' he replied. 'The general public don't like us much.'

'But they like you, especially the girls and you're a Kiwi, that's kind of neutral.'

Simon looked serious. 'What can I tell you about the Jebbs killings?'

Dave fell in with the new mood. This was what he had come for. 'Can you tell me anything about HMP Yaltham Hill?'

'Ah, the perv's nick. That's largely off limits to the likes of us. They don't let the press within a mile of the place.'

Yes, thought Dave. That was probably one reason why Jones got away with impunity when supplying innocent young kids. Yaltham Hill was the secure prison for convicted paedophiles situated just outside the bounds of this city. Jones had worked there before being summarily transferred to Hampshire. It all smelt of a cover up.

'The prison officer called Jones worked there, and he's suspected of smuggling kids inside for the pervs to play with.'

Simon nodded. 'We know. We've heard the gossip, but the

authorities are so tight lipped.'

'That hasn't worked; the rumours are rife everywhere.'

'I know. We think Jones should have been arrested.'

Dave wondered. 'He must have been charmed or someone was protecting him.'

Simon was angry now. 'Feeding kids to evil perverts. If it's true he deserved to be killed.'

'Can't argue with that, but if someone was protecting him. Christ – who would bother to do that?'

Simon withdrew some papers from a file. 'Well, the man was bent but he had a funny background for a prison officer. Our crime desk has had some confidential stuff from within the paedophile world. Jones was a guy from a wealthy background: public school, the lot, but it's reckoned he was a pervert as well. If he was being protected well look at this. Here's who his uncle is and here's his real father.'

Dave to the proffered sheet of paper. He was startled but not all that surprised. He had a breakthrough that seemed to have avoided the police and it led back to the south coast where all this had begun. Should he tell the police? Well, yes, but why should he? The authorities had behaved disgracefully in protecting Jones and that's what it amounted to. Yes, he must reveal what he'd discovered, but not yet.

He drank a second cup of coffee and chatted sport for a while. Then he said goodbye to Simon and left. As he left the building he switched his mobile phone on. He was mortified to find that Josie had been trying to contact him for twelve hours. He answered and steeled himself for a telling off.

CHAPTER 21

Dave found Tom ready and waiting in Weston-Super-Mare and told him what Josie had said.

'I know all about it,' said Tom. 'Emily called me as well. No recriminations, you'd both better stay at our place for a day or so.'

'We'd be very grateful. Josie can lie low for a few days while we get the police involved.'

Tom spoke. 'Are you any further forward with things?'

'No sure. But I learned stuff today that could be very revealing.'

'All right. I won't lean on you to tell me. It's just that it is so unsettling, what with Ollavasen business and now this. Em and me feel terribly for Lorraine. Lorraine delivered little Peter into the world and now Emily's expecting again.'

It was late evening when Tom turned his car into the short lane to his house. They had kept in touch with their wives via mobile phone throughout the day but it had been an anxious few hours. Josie's car was parked and they found the two girls watching television with Peter in his special chair beside them. Emily leapt to her feet and hugged both men.

'I've made up the bed in the spare room,' said Emily 'You and Josie must stay here until it's safe for you to go back to London.'

'I've told the police about the message,' said Josie. 'Not much interest though, as you'd expect.'

'They've told the London Met but they obviously think it's a hoax,' said Emily.

'No,' said Josie. 'That voice wasn't a joker. It was deliberately distorted. The threat was real.'

'Maybe I'd better tell the Banner that I'm not working on this story any more,' said Dave.

Josie looked shocked. 'What about Lorraine? You can't walk away just now. The police are getting nowhere but you say you've found something.'

'Well, I am not getting into the classic dilemma where the detective's girl is abducted. Josie, while I'm involved in this mess I suggest you go stay with my folks in Auckland.'

Josie flushed. 'Not bloody likely. I won't run away. You can stuff

New Zealand. I'm going nowhere.' She glared and flounced out of the room and into the kitchen.

Dave moved to follow her but Tom caught his arm. 'No, Dave. I'm sure you're right but let Emily talk to her.'

Emily gave them both a wan smile and followed Josie. The two girls were in the kitchen for almost a quarter of an hour. The men could hear subdued conversation but no clear idea of what was said.

Then both emerged and they saw that Josie had been crying. 'Emily's talked to me,' she said. 'She's so convincing – a proper lawyer. But you're right. I can still work on my book over there and it will be warmer won't it?'

Dave grinned. 'It will be a whole lot warmer. Long days warm seas and sunshine. And what's more when I've done here I will be joining you.'

'I don't like this, not one little bit,' said Inspector Marchway. 'That recording was too sophisticated. Our people say the voice distortion was done with equipment you won't find outside the film industry.'

'Do we think this Mrs Manning is in danger?' asked Super-intendent Hollins.

'That's what it looks like. I wish that stupid Kiwi reporter would come forward and talk to us. He's a meddler, but he may have found something we need to know.'

'Yes, bloody press. All that hacking and nosing into celebrities' lives. We can't do any of that.' Marchway looked gloomy. 'We've had a report on the Ternby killing. Cold blooded and done with a heavy bar to the back of the skull – just like the Blake-Grass one. That's the problem. Was Blake-Grass the man behind the Sussex murders and did Ternby know too much?'

'We have to work on facts, but if I were to guess I would say yes to both of those propositions.'

Mulberry Yacht Charters had moved from the wooden building in Mulberry Lane to plush offices in Woolston, Southampton. Dave had decided the time had come to find Richard Halderholm. He had met the man just once during the Ollavasen affair and he doubted if he could pull off the deception he'd worked last time when he pretended to be a customer. Dave had checked and it seemed Halderholm was still running the Mediterranean charters, but the firm had been bought out by Yachtiegear, awful name.

Yachtiegear was run by Ifor Harris-Evans, and was a chain of boat chandlery shops established in most coastal areas of the UK. The interesting connection was that twenty percent of the shares in Yachtiegear were owned by the late Graham Blake-Grass. The remainder belonged to Ifor Harris-Evans the firm's founder. Dave had checked up on the New Zealand angle, He remembered hearing or reading the name Blake-Grass in Auckland. He had then discovered that Bigarse was directly funding two branches of Yachtiegear in New Zealand, one in each island. He would ask Josie to find out more when she arrived in Auckland.

Dave had met Ifor several times. He was a laidback self-made businessman of a type familiar to anyone from New Zealand or Australia. The man was Welsh, from a land where rugby was almost a religion and that suited Dave. Otherwise he knew little about that country although he had sailed there once in a dinghy meet. Josie had told him that Wales was an ancient nation much put upon by the English. The people loved playing rugby, singing and a local language was still spoken. He warmed to this; these Welsh seemed very like Maoris. Ifor seemed a decent guy although the evil Jones, it appeared, was Welsh, but with a name like that he probably had to be. Dave grinned – he was learning more and more about the Brits as each day went by. But he needed to check on the information about Jones that Simon Ormerod had given him in Bristol. If that was true it would be a revelation.

'David Manning, good to see you,' said Ifor. 'I always read your bits in the yacht press. My colleague Richard Halderholm says I'm not to call you an Australian.'

'Not likely,' Dave laughed. 'I wouldn't call you an Englishman. Not that I'm really down on Aussies. They just tend to be a bit loud.'

'That's the opposite from the English. They say we Welsh talk too much, but we never know what they're thinking. David, that's not why you're here – you've been asking a lot of questions.'

'That's the Kiwi in me. I admit I'm a nosy bastard.'

Ifor stared at Dave. His mood had swung. 'You've been nosing all right: asking questions about Bigarse.'

'Only in so far as it affects a friend of my wife and mine, Wallace Markham. As you know he was brutally killed and his wife Lorraine is in grief.'

'Very well; I've no doubt the Daily Banner are on the case.'

Dave knew he was in for a grilling. 'They have resources that can help me. But I only have authority to search matters relating to sailing. Wally Markham and his wife were sailors. I don't know about any of the other victims. Mr Blake-Grass was into motor yachts, the man Jebbs took pictures of yachts. I don't know if the other man Jones sailed.'

Ifor nodded. 'I would think it unlikely. Have you found anything about Jones?'

'Only that he was wholly corrupt and involved in child abuse.'

'Jones was Welsh born in Cardiff. We are a God-fearing people but even we cannot avoid the odd Jones in our midst.'

'Was Jebbs a Welshman?'

'Most certainly not,' Ifor for the first time looked displeased.

'Sorry, no offence. I'm only asking because when he was lynched our friend was killed and Wally was a decent guy.'

Ifor looked at his watch. 'Have you considered a racist motive? Markham was married to a black woman.'

'Lorraine is certainly mixed race but she's a medical professional. A public servant, as was her husband.'

Ifor looked at his watch again. 'I have been very patient with you, Mr Manning, but there are limits and time is money as I'm sure you understand.'

'All right, I won't waste any more of it. May I speak to Richard Halderholm?'

'Unfortunately he's not available today.'

'Well, I've no choice but drop him in the shit. Jebbs made porno videos and Halderholm acted in one…'

Ifor stood up and now he was really angry. 'That is outrageous – where's your proof?'

Dave reached in an inner pocket and flicked the Everett CD onto Ifor's desk. 'There's your proof. Jebbs shot this and he was alleged to be deeply religious. Make sense of that.'

Next morning the snow was back, an overnight blizzard had blocked the roads for miles and filled the lane leading to Emily and Tom's cottage.

Dave and Josie were gloomy. Josie had been reconciled to her trip to New Zealand, now it seemed reaching Heathrow was as attainable as landing on the moon. Dave had somehow obtained a cut price ticket for an indirect flight in six days time.

Tom stared out of the window at the white countryside. 'If villains are after you people they'll need a helicopter to get here.'

'Bigarse owned one of those with a tame pilot,' said Dave.

Emily came into the sitting room. 'Phone line's dead and I can't access my emails,' she complained. 'I don't know if it's any help, but I've a stack of photocopies of stuff in the CD package that was seized from Ferdy Modlington. We didn't have to use them in the end, only the really nasty ones, but these were taken by Jebbs, they were definitely his camera.'

'Are these boats?' asked Dave.

'No, they all seem to be country scenes but these six are of children with an adult, probably a teacher.' She laid them out on a table.

Dave sorted through them and then studied one intensely. 'Oh God, there was me thinking I'd hit a blank wall and maybe could go back home with Josie and now I'm right back in it again.'

'How come?' asked Tom.

Dave handed him the picture. 'This one has got Jebbs' logo. So, what do you see?'

Tom looked puzzled. 'I see a bunch of young kids being shown a historic ship. That's the *SS Great Britain* so it must be Bristol docks. I've been there when I was at uni.'

'There's a bit more to it,' said Dave. 'I want to know who those kids are and the name of the girl teacher. And I know the guy standing with them. He will be able to answer my questions. He's only just down the road and I can't reach him today nor probably tomorrow either.' He punched his left hand in frustration.

CHAPTER 22

The Harris-Evans executive mansion on the edge of the hills at East Meon had originally been a farmhouse and as such was easily cut off from the world by snow, fallen trees or any similar natural phenomenon. Jasmine was always amused when her husband foretold the weather better than the weather men on the telly. He had phoned her yesterday and told her that snow was on the way and that he would be staying in the hotel he owned in Southsea. Provided he was not with that horrible skinny little secretary girl she didn't mind.

Tomorrow was Sunday so she wouldn't have to drag her sister to the Cymraig Forgather chapel. Ifor's religious devotion was a classic doctrine of the: don't do as I do – do as I say. Cerise was still with them and flitted around the house saying little between spasms of inconsolable grief. Jasmine was determined that once Graham was safely buried or cremated they would find Cerise a new man who could cherish her and maybe give her the children she never had from her husband. She was still young enough at thirty-eight but her time was running out.

Ifor had requested her – no, that wasn't true. Ifor had ordered her: that was more like it. Ifor had ordered her to check his incoming emails. As the phone lines were down that wasn't much use. Ifor had taken his mobile phone with him, but this was a heaven-sent opportunity for her to check up on him over the last few weeks. She went into his private office. This was an inner sanctum where she was not normally allowed. The daily help cleaned it but that lady wouldn't know how to access a computer anyway.

She switched on the third of the computers, the one Ifor used rather covertly. She found nothing particularly compromising; maybe he'd erased anything she might look at.

Anyway, she would do her duty and check the Yachtiegear business mails. And they were deadly dull; all order lists for paint, outboard motors and rope line. One mail a while back was a puzzle. It came from Ifor's new office in New Zealand.

We've put your Poms to work on light duties and driving. They know fuck all about boats.

That sounded like a Kiwi or an Aussie. Tell it as it is. She rather liked that. She remembered that hunky Kiwi sports writer who was around the sailing scene with a gorgeous girl friend. He was Dave something – she couldn't remember the rest.

She wandered through the house and then, through the glass patio door, she saw a fox in the garden. She flung the door open but quickly shut it with the extra aid of the icy blast that swept down from the hills.

'There's a lot of pictures of kids, but they look harmless enough,' Dave passed the copies to Josie.

'No, I can't see anything too harmful,' she said. 'They're fully clothed and having genuine fun.'

'There's no evidence that Jebbs was a pervert. He shot those adult porno videos but that was probably for hard cash.'

'What do we know about Jebbs' ex that he killed?' asked Josie.

'That's the connection to Bigarse. The Banner has traced her to a mother, one of his girls and it seems he was the father. But they must have got it together when they were both in their teens.'

'So it all points to him; Bigarse that is. What about the other people Jebbs killed?'

In spite of everything Dave grinned. 'One was a woman politician. Divorced, rich and cut her husband out of her business. Brave girl though, she died trying to get the gun away.'

'Politician? Hmm, no great loss. Did Jebbs have some vendetta there?'

Dave was doubtful. 'He's dead as well, so he can't help us. But it doesn't make sense. If Jebbs wanted to get rid of his ex he could have done something much more subtle. But he kills six people in broad daylight and having done that gives himself up. Even if he was a psycho it doesn't make sense.'

Josie held up her mobile phone. 'I've got a good signal now. Do you want to ring up the man in that photo?'

Dave nearly said yes, but something irrational maybe told him no. 'I think it's time I made a date to talk to the local police.'

'That reporter Manning wants to talk to us again.' Chief Inspector Marchway reported to his boss. 'What do we say?'

Superintendent Hollins frowned. 'I'll see him. Remember, last time we ignored him only to find he was one jump ahead of us.'

'All right, tell him to get here in the next hour.'

Marchway shook his head. 'Sorry, sir, but he says he's snowed in somewhere near Alresford.'

81

'Just tell him to get here as soon as he can.'

'I'll do that, sir. Bloody reporters. Why do they meddle like this?'

Hollins smiled and clicked the computer mouse. 'Well, he won't have seen this. This is the prison report by the psychiatrist who talked to Jebbs.'

Marchway glared. 'Blow them. The man was evil, just plain evil.'

'Yes, but take a look at this. *The prisoner, Jebbs was a driven man. Driven by religion...*'

'Oh, yes,' Marchway laughed. 'Religious, and the man made porno films.'

'No, listen.' *Jebbs was bitterly offended by his ex-wife's lack of faith and felt her leaving the marriage to be a breach of religious duty. His ex-wife, Ms Furness, was concerned with educating children from a care home. Some of these children had been cruelly molested sexually. We are satisfied that Ms Furness had no part in any of this and may not have known about it. Jebbs in his mental state believed she was involved and that she had to be purged.* 'That's it, Dennis, take it or leave it, but it does explain a lot.'

'Sounds a load of shit to me.'

'Very likely, but we do not let this reporter, Manning see a word of this report.'

'Yes, sir. God help us if the Daily Banner caught hold of that.'

The farmer had arrived at first light and cleared the snow drifts. They were not the massive obstructions of the first fall, but still enough to block all the approaches to the cottage. Dave had worried about the level of antifreeze in the car after the record drop in temperature. Josie's car was little driven outside London. In fact there was not a problem and the engine ran sweetly. The tiny Nissan was an ideal town car but it slithered all over the place on the icy lane. Dave reached the main road and turned for Winchester. Five minutes later a white transit van overtook him and then clinically and expertly forced him off the road onto the snow covered grass verge. Dave seethed with fury. He was not given to road rage but this was just too blatant even if the road did have a vestige of ice.

'What the hell,' he shouted.

Then his driver door was wrenched open and two gloved hands pulled him off his seat.

He looked up and saw two black-covered figures both with face covering and the one holding him had a podgy obese waistline.

'Oh, fuck it,' said a muffled voice. 'It's the fellah – not the girlie.'

Dave was shocked now. This was Josie's car but how would these men know she would be driving in it? Well, evidently they had that wrong. Dave was lean and fit: a sailor and a rugby player. If this fat slob intended to abduct him then he was in for a fight and a half.

It seemed the slob guessed this. 'Boy, you ask too many questions. Stop it, or next time we take your girl – see!'

Dave slumped back on his seat, but angry as he was, he checked the registration number of the van as it drove away. P47LBK. That was one advantage of being a journalist: one remembered these things. He stood up and walked around the car. It was undamaged and with a little bit of care he should be able to push her back on the road. He let off the brake and holding the steering wheel through the open window he heaved as only a Kiwi rugby forward can. The car slid off the short banking and returned to the road. Then he found his mobile phone and called the police and then Josie.

'Darling, if anyone comes to the door hide. Don't answer it. There's some nasty people around. Can you put Tom on now?'

CHAPTER 23

'Don't know what to make about Manning's road incident,' Inspector Marchway was giving his morning report to his chief. 'That transit van had false plates. The number Manning wrote down belonged to an old Renault written off in an accident in North Hampshire.' He laughed. 'You'd never believe the cheek, but the plates were nicked a few days later from our own secure pound at Alton.'

'There'll be some red faces when that news reaches them,' Hollins replied. 'I take it Manning's not a glory seeker; that he's telling the truth.'

'Yes, sir. I asked our officers from the scene and they're convinced he's telling the truth. He thinks they wanted to abduct his wife. It was her car you see.'

Hollins was concerned now. 'That's Josephine Manning. She was the target of that phone threat.'

'Yes, sir. Our technicians are still working on the recording to see if they can identify the voice and trace the source.'

'One advantage of Manning being a bloody journo is that he remembers things. The assailants hardly said anything and they were dressed in black but he says one was definitely well overweight. You know, sir. Fat and sweaty.'

'Sounds like a white van man anyway,' Hollins sighed.

'Yes, sir, but it was a white transit that was involved in the Sussex lynchings.'

'So are a quarter of all the vehicles on the road. Can't see that helping us much.'

'They were waiting for me,' Dave was angry. 'How the hell could they know I was going out in Josie's car?'

'All right,' said Tom. 'Let me have a look at that car.'

The Nissan was parked on the narrow roadside outside the cottage. Tom borrowed the keys and climbed inside. Then he opened the engine cover and the boot. Next he stared inside and probed in both compartments. Finally he put a waterproof on the icy ground and wriggled under the rear bumper. 'Gotcha,' he yelled. 'Thought so. Come look at this little beauty.' He emerged grinning with a tiny round cylindrical object in his gloved hand.

84

'Tom, what is it?' asked Josie who had joined them.

'It's a tracker. Taped to the chassis. Spin off from the satnav. My company make them. Dave, you should know all about them. I bet Sid Everett in his phone hacking days would've loved to use one.'

'So, they would know where the car was.' Dave looked baffled. 'They must have planted that in London. Christ, we're up against some clever and well organised people.'

'That's it. As soon as you turned on the electrics and started the engine they'd be in business.'

'And they were waiting close by.' Dave felt a shiver of cold. 'I need to get Josie to New Zealand right now.'

Two days later Dave drove the car, now minus the tracker, to Heathrow and saw Josie safely on the cheap budget flight to New Zealand. He had called his parents and they had been very happy to give her hospitality. They had always made it plain that Josie might be a Brit or a Pom, but they loved her and fully approved of his choice. Dave had not told them the real reason for this visit, but he had concocted a story about her looking for a holiday property. This was partly true but not yet attainable on their pay. It was a dream for the future.

He drove back to Alresford wondering what his next move should be. He would have the house to himself today, apart from Lily and Peter. He had stopped in London to buy Peter a little miniature sledge. He still had no idea of the gender of their own unborn child. Josie was very traditional and declined to have a scan. He parked the car and sighed with relief.

'Dave,' called Lily. 'Just had the police on the phone. They want you to talk to them about the other day,' her voice dropped to a delighted whisper. 'It's the car jacking you went through. I can't think what things are coming to. First this mad person that snatches Peter, now this.'

'I know, Lily, it's a wicked world.'

'Yes, but this is Hampshire. It didn't never happen before.'

'First of all you'd better take charge of this.' Dave handed Inspector Marchway the tracking device. 'We found it underneath the car. My friend Tom works for the firm that make them.'

Marchway rolled the tiny object through his fingers. 'They make them for the military and for us. They wouldn't normally be in circulation.' He put the tracker on the table. 'Right, Mr Manning. I want an exact description of those two men who attacked you.'

'Not easy, they were dressed head to foot in black, but one, the guy who spoke was fat; bulged in all sorts of places.'

'What about the way he spoke? I mean posh or regional accent.'

'Sorry, but I'm not from the UK. I mean all these regional accent wars. We don't have any of that where I come from.'

Marchway laughed. 'Oh yes, what happens when we Brits think you're an Aussie?'

Dave laughed. 'Touché is the term isn't it?'

'I'll let you know something in confidence. Not for the Daily Banner.'

Dave nodded. 'It'll be confidential – go ahead.'

'The prison transport driver who witnessed the Sussex murders described one of the thugs as obese.'

'Old bigarse was large,' said Dave. 'But he's dead. Might've been him in Sussex but not the one who threatened me. Tell you something; the guy was prepared to snatch a girl but when I started to turn awkward they pissed off sharpish.'

'So, you didn't think you were in physical danger?' asked Marchway.

'Not really and the fat smelly bloke didn't seem much of a threat.'

'Smelly?'

Dave grinned. 'Well, perfume; scent not sweat. Could be a poofter.'

'Now,' said Marchway. 'We are drifting into dangerous territory.'

'I know, politically incorrect. We don't go for that so much down under.'

Sam Pollingham examined the two pictures that Dave had dropped on his desk. 'Yes, I remember these being taken. God, are you telling me the man with camera was Jebbs?'

''Fraid so. Do you know the name of the teacher with the kids?'

'Not sure. You see I'm a ship designer: naval architect is what we used to be called. I get asked to show kids around famous old ships. I do *HMS Victory* of course and I've done the *Belfast* on the Thames. But that was my first tour of *SS Great Britain* as a guide.'

'Would you know where the kids came from?'

'Not sure, but I've an idea it was from outside Bristol. They came in a coach from a firm in Yeovil.' Sam Pollingham looked concerned. 'Is this connected with Jebbs?'

'We're not sure, but these photos were found in the possession of a man recently put on the sex offenders register.'

'I don't like the sound of that, but would a pervert like these pictures? They look pretty innocent to me.'

Dave was not sure himself how relevant all this was. 'As I said, I'm not digging for dirt. I'm only searching to see if any of this relates to the boat scene.'

Sam looked troubled. 'I told the police this, but I don't know how much notice they took. The morning that Jebbs was killed I was due to meet Blake-Grass and Darren Ternby to measure up some modifications to BG's yacht engine room. It's just that neither of them turned up at the time agreed and I never saw either for another twenty-four hours.

CHAPTER 24

Josie arrived at Auckland Airport at two p.m. in the afternoon – UK time, and therefore in the pitch dark of night in New Zealand. She was stiff and bleary eyed from the long flight but followed the crowd to passport control. So swift had been her departure from England that nothing had been done to obtain an entry visa and this worried her. She had been taken aside for questioning but it had all been friendly and she had explained that she was the wife of a New Zealand citizen. She had then been startled to find that her husband was a national name. 'A writer and a fine sportsman...' The customs lady had smiled. Her entry had been promptly stamped and she had been released.

It was still far too early for her to reach Dave's parents so she found a nice all night café and settled down to read the local papers over coffee and a tasty bacon sandwich. She liked this country. Josie had travelled much of the world in her student days but New Zealand always came across as the most familiar of the English speaking countries, certainly more so than the United States. She had a brief from Dave to visit one of the Auckland branches of Yachtiegear, the chandlery and boat equipment suppliers linked to Graham Blake-Grass's empire. Sailing and all water sports were a national passion with Kiwis, ranking second behind rugby. With a bit of luck she would get some on-water delight with her parents-in-law. She liked both Joe and Helen. They had accepted her into their family with joy and genuine friendship. Dave's teenage sister, Maggie was likeable and played the piano rather well. Josie was determined not to overstay her welcome but she could not return home to the UK until Dave was satisfied that she was safe to do so.

An hour after first light she to out the mobile phone that Dave had given her and rang his parents. Joe and Helen lived in the smart Auckland suburb of Parnell. They owned a fine Victorian style house that could have been duplicated in any English country town. Joe was about to leave for his office but he diverted to pick up Josie and run her back to their house. Helen gave her a hug and kiss and showed her to her room for the stay. With huge relief Josie took a shower and then changed into shorts, flip-flops and a colourful flowing sun top that camouflaged her now just visible baby bump. Thank goodness the

English bitter winter was thousands of miles away and she could enjoy the sunshine.

'Dave, Josie's arrived in Auckland.' Tom called from his computer. 'Email's just come through. She says it's hot and sunny,'
Emily laughed. 'I suppose you do have winter sometimes?'
'You bet,' Dave replied. 'You should see our ski resorts. Could I see that mail and I'll send one back.'
Dave was relieved. Josie was out of reach of whoever was orchestrating these killings. He could get on with his investigation with this worry gone. Where was he to look next?
Yes, the miscreant Jones. There was no evidence that Jones had ever been in a boat in his life, but somehow Dave felt the man was a key factor in the mystery. What did they know about Jones? The man was Welsh by birth, but that mustn't be allowed to be any sort of stigma. Dave himself was too used to being thought an Australian and a subject for comedy. Jones was a corrupt prison officer and, much worse, he was suspected of paedophile inclinations and, even worse than that, to have supplied children to a sex offender's prison. So, why hadn't he been exposed and arrested? Was he being protected? Last puzzle; who had selected Jones as guard for Jebbs on that fatal day? Well, probably the police might know but they would never confide in him. He would phone the Banner crime desk and report that he had reached an impasse. With any luck they would release him and let him join his wife in Auckland. No, that wouldn't do. He owed a duty to Lorraine. He wouldn't put undue pressure on the girl in her grief but there were things he needed to know.

Cerise drove her smart four-by-four away from Jasmine's house and headed south. At last she felt able to return to her own, or rather Graham's luxurious house, just outside Lymington on the edge of the New Forest. She loved the wide expanse of the forest and loved to go riding there. She had kept in touch with the house staff and the girl who groomed and fed her horses. She had worried almost as much about her horses, as she did for poor Graham and that made her feel guilty. The roads had now been cleared and gritted and she could hear the rattle of the gravel in her car mudguards. It was bitterly cold outside but warm in the car. She regretted that there would be no trips to the Swiss ski slopes this winter. She understood from the house staff that the police had searched the place and taken away several bin liners of stuff. Bloody cheek, when they hadn't consulted her and

89

failed to produce any warrant. She understood this had happened when she was being questioned by that stupid copper.

Graham's body would not be released for burial for another couple of weeks at least, or so the police had told her. Then she must grit her teeth and make arrangements for a burial or a cremation. Graham had left an elaborate will in her favour but as a man who thought himself immortal he hadn't declared any funeral preference. She reached Oyster Bay House, their home, and found the wrought-iron gates closed. She left the cosy security of her car and typed in the security pass number. The gates swung open and she drove on to the house. She parked and went first to say hello to her horses. They were happy, thank goodness munching their top quality hay. Then she found her front door key.

and went indoors. It was almost as cold indoors as in the outside world. Cerise found the heating controls and turned them up to a full blast. Whatever the national situation she could afford it. She went to Graham's office and was not surprised to find the police had removed his main computer. Next, she went to the fake drinks cabinet and pressed the concealed latch. It swung open to reveal the heavy safe door. Months ago she had secretly acquired the combination code. She had suspected Graham of receiving letters from a mistress but had had to admit her paranoia when she found nothing. There had been an odd file box in there as well but she hadn't bothered with it and apart from this the safe was empty. The safe door opened on command and there it was. Cerise slid the box out and took it across to the desk. Most of the few papers within were written in some sort of number code. No not all; she stiffened with shock as she read the final one. So that was it. Why hadn't she guessed before?

'Wallace's funeral is on Thursday,' Lorraine's mother told them. 'You will come please. We want all their friends to come and give her support.'

'Of course we will,' Emily hugged her.

Emily, Tom and Dave had driven to East Hampshire once more. Dave needed to talk to Lorraine and Emily was anxious that he be tactful. With Josie overseas now she felt Dave needed watching. They had noticed that his journalistic hunting sense had become blatant in the last few days. Tact was needed more than ever if Lorraine was to survive this nightmare and go on to better things.

'Emily, can we talk?' It was Lorraine. She had entered the room quietly and was standing beside a few feet away.

'Of course,' she replied.

'Come in the kitchen then. It's nice and quiet there. I drove the kids back to their school first thing but I've got to be back there at three. Until then we've got time to talk.'

Emily followed Lorraine into the room. Dave was with Lorraine's parents. He stared after them but didn't try to follow. The kitchen was a large, well lit space with a table and chairs. Lorraine pointed Emily to the table and then made them both a cup of coffee. 'Just right for a cold day,' she smiled.

'How are the children?' Emily asked.

'They miss Wally terribly, but they wanted to go back to school to see their friends. The school have been great – really sympathetic and helpful. Emily I need to talk.'

Emily nodded and waited.

'Emily, Wally was terribly moody and worried for the few days before he died. He knew something terrible was going to happen but he wouldn't talk to me. In fact he screamed at me and he'd never done that before.'

Emily said nothing but waited.

'I told you all how he shouted about Bigarse in his sleep.'

'Yes.'

'Well, I went back to our house after taking the kids to school. That was yesterday and I found this tucked away on Wally's desk.' Lorraine held up a rumpled sheet of paper. 'I'd rather you read it first. You're a lawyer and Dave's a journalist…'

Emily smiled. 'And Tom's an electronic geek. Much better keep the secret among the girls.'

'I know, but I'll have to pass this to the police.' She handed the paper to Emily.

B.G. Jones, Ternby and Paul Fatso Ferresier. If anything happens to me tell the law.
Wallace Markham.

'I don't know if this is relevant but Wally was frightened or apprehensive that morning. He hugged the kids and me and I thought he was about to cry.' Lorraine was dabbing her own eyes.

Emily looked up and saw that Dave had come into the room and she was annoyed. She glared at him and shook her head vigorously.

Dave ignored her but spoke very gently, his voice little more than a whisper. 'Lorri', who is Paul Ferresier?'

'He's a man who works for Yachtiegear in Southampton. I met him with Wally in that shop. He's a fat slob.'

Emily intervened. 'Then there's Amanda Furness, the girl Jebbs murdered. She was B-G's daughter. There's got to be a connection.'

'More than likely,' said Dave. 'And Amanda's second husband is alive and living in Bristol. Sorry, Lorri, but all this is going to need checking.'

'I know,' said Lorraine. 'I will have to give this to the police, but I'll scan you a copy as well.' She paused and frowned. 'Dave, will the police take this seriously or will they laugh at me?'

'No they won't. They're very sympathetic and what's more they're not getting anywhere with this tragedy.'

CHAPTER 25

Josie missed her husband. She missed his company in bed and his laughter and even his more irritating habits. Joe and Helen treated her as another daughter; she was fully part of the family but she still missed Dave. The weather was a delight apart from one sub-tropical storm that she had rather enjoyed watching. She had crewed for Joe in two races in his thirty-five foot keelboat. New Zealand men were never in the forefront of gender equality and she had been gratified that Joe had thought her a useful crew member. Dave's younger sister Maggie was away at university in Australia so Josie had been allowed to use the battered old Honda that Maggie drove on holiday. She had been issued with a short-term driving licence and had not been required to take a test. Auckland's streets were crowded at all times but the rural roads round and about were undisturbed, at least by UK standards.

On the fourth day of her visit she found her way to the Yachtiegear store on the waterfront. Dave wanted her opinion of the place, and he had asked her to buy some tins of varnish for the little dinghy they had hired for the Auckland summer. She only hoped Dave would be there, plus brush to apply it. She found the new store with its brightly painted shop front and warehouse behind. She went in and ordered the varnish and paid with her own credit card and Dave's Yachtiegear bonus card. The assistant was a smartly dressed man who must have been a recent immigrant. He spoke English with a trace of a Dorset accent. The man was polite and helpful. He directed another obese and surly man who carried the paint tins, stacking them in the boot of the Honda.

'Ifor,' Cerise's voice had an air of both sweetness and menace. 'What did you know about Graham's plans? Did you know someone was out to get him?'

Ifor grimaced. 'I owed Bigarse money, it's true, but we had it sorted. Cerise, I don't kill people even it is tempting sometimes.'

Cerise brushed aside a tear. 'I wish you wouldn't call Graham that. He was a fitness fanatic and he had a fit body. Not like some people not a thousand miles from here.' She glared at Ifor.

Jasmine intervened to keep the peace. 'Yes, Ifor enjoys his grub and maybe he doesn't take enough exercise. But look, Cerise. We've offered you hospitality in your bad time and I don't think you should be throwing wild accusations around.'

'All right. See what I found in our safe at home.' She dropped the file box on the table in front of Ifor.

'Watch out, you nearly spilt my drink,' he glowered. He opened the box and sifted through the papers. 'This is all some sort of code cipher. You'll need an expert if you want to make sense of it.'

'No it's this email. Read it!' Cerise snapped. 'No, I'll read it to you.'

Email from Paul Ferresier. Mission complete. Well done you. Iver, the skipper and J T. .

Cerise glared.

Ifor yawned. 'So what? It doesn't tell us what this mission was. Your old man was involved in business. You get cryptic emails all the time. Let me have a look.' He to the paper and laughed. 'Girl, my name is Ifor not Iver. Graham and I did business. He knew how to spell my name. And look at the date girl, that's months ago.'

'Maybe whoever sent the email didn't know how your name is spelt.'

Ifor groaned. 'I've never had dealings with that address. Look it's *grasshopper@supermail.com* – doesn't even give a name.'

'I will have to tell the police.'

'I doubt they'll take any notice. From all I've heard they haven't a clue – no pun intended.'

'No Cerise,' Jasmine intervened. 'You don't want the police questioning you again and getting suspicious. I tell you what. Our shop manager in Southampton says there's a yacht journalist sniffing around the case. He's that Manning who they say put the police on the trail of the Ollavasen murder...'

'Ollavasen,' Ifor laughed. 'He was no loss by all accounts.'

'No,' Jasmine continued, 'Go and find this David Manning and talk to him. I bet he's more idea of what's been going on than the police.'

'Tom, you technology communications geeks do amazing things. What do I owe you for this long-distance call to NZ?'

Tom laughed. 'I've no idea until we get the next phone bill.'

'Let me know when you do. As I say I've just talked to Josie in

Auckland. Strewth, twelve thousand miles away and it's as clear as if she was in the next room.'

'How is she?'

'She says she misses me and well, I'm really missing her. But she's done some sailing and she asked about the yachtiegear shop for me. She's been told that the assistants in there are Poms. Anyway she's getting on fine with my people and my Sis, Maggie is home on vacation.'

'By the way,' said Tom. 'Your Daily Banner called. The man was very apologetic but said you weren't answering your mobile.'

Dave laughed. 'No it's switched off and in my briefcase.' He sighed, '. I'll call them.' Dave left the room to recover his phone.

He returned a few minutes later with an odd expression on his face. 'Well I never. Bigarse's widow wants a word with me. Says the cops won't listen to her.'

Dave had arranged to meet Cerise Blake-Grass at a remote pub in the middle of nowhere. It was called *The Pub With No Name* and that was not a lot of help in trying to find it. In the end he borrowed a spare satnav from Tom. In truth the pub was a delight. It stood on hills in part of the highest ground in Hampshire amidst woods and fields that made him think of home. The roads had been cleared of snow right up to the pub car park which seemed to prove that this was a popular place. He climbed out of the little Nissan and shivered in the icy East wind blast. Only a handful of cars were already parked which was hardly surprising in this weather. Nearby was a very clean and spruce red four-by-four. The rear number plate read BG 6. Not much doubt who that was.

Inside the pub it was warm and very snug. This was so typically English and a million miles from the drinking dens back home. Suddenly he felt hungry as he smelt the scents of roast from the kitchen. He was in a low ceiling wood-beamed bar with framed hunting scenes on the walls and dark wood tables and chairs. Sitting at one of the tables sipping a glass of white wine was a remarkably pretty dark-haired girl.

The girl looked up and smiled. 'You must be David?'

'That's right, I'm David Manning and you must be…'

'Yeah, I'm Cerise.' She stared around and dropped her voice. 'We really need to talk.'

Dave could still smell the delicious scents. 'How about some lunch?' he suggested.

'Yeah, I would like that; haven't been eating too well lately.'

'I understand. You've had a terrible tragedy. My condolences.'

'Thanks, David. It's been awful, but I'll get over it.'

Dave had been discreetly sizing up this girl. Girl she was: maybe just thirty. Her late husband must have been mid-sixties or more. Yes, slim figure, shapely breasts beneath her fashion jumper. He assumed the old fellow had appreciated all this.

'Come on, Mrs Blake-Grass. There's no one in that dining room. Let's eat and talk.'

She smiled, 'And David, please call me Cerise.'

Cerise handed Dave the scanned copy of the email she'd found; it certainly was an odd coincidence. 'Do you know if your husband had any big business deal on track? he asked. 'Could that just possibly be the mission complete,'

'Yes, I had considered that, but the message comes from this Paul F and I've no idea who he is or what he is.'

Dave suddenly felt a pulse of excitement. Could this possibly be? If it was, then he might have a breakthrough. 'Cerise, I know you must be anxious to protect your husband's good name…'

Suddenly she laughed, but there was no humour in it. 'Look, I miss poor Graham terribly. You know I saw his dead body not long after it happened. The police thought I'd done it but, no way! I'd never hurt Graham, not however many dodgy deals he was into or how many fancy girls he was screwing.' Now she was crying: sobbing into a tiny handkerchief. Dave tactfully looked down and studied the menu card. 'Sorry, David, don't take any notice of me.'

'No,' he replied. 'Let it all go. It's the best way.'

'I know,' she said. 'I'll be better in a minute.'

'Yes, take it easy. Talk when you're ready,'

Cerise put away her handkerchief. 'No it's all right. I want to talk – get this out in the open.' She paused as the waitress brought their soup and bread rolls.

Dave waited until they were undisturbed. 'Tell me, Cerise, do you know who the people in this email are; Paul F for one.'

She shook her head. 'No, but my brother-in-law is called Ifor and he borrowed money from my husband for his business. But he spells his name as Ifor not Iver. He's Welsh you see.'

'Would that be the company called Yachtiegear?'

'Yes, but I don't think Ifor was the person the message mentions. In fact I tackled him about it last night and he denied it,' she paused. 'Well, you know when someone's telling the truth? I can always tell and this time he was.'

'So, you've no idea who Iver is or Paul F?'

'No, I only wish I did.' She stared at him. 'Must I give this to the police?'

'Yes, you must and do it today.'

'If you say so. There's that horrid Inspector man. He thought I'd done it – killed my Graham. Well I didn't – not true.' Now she was dabbing tears again.

'Here, take this,' he said handing her his spare hankie. 'It's clean. I haven't used it.' He spoke gently now. 'Eat your food. I promise no more questions.'

It might have seemed a wasted encounter but not so. Dave had an intuition that was rapidly expanding into a real idea. It was just possible he had the breakthrough that everyone else had missed.

Dave's sister, Maggie was a tall athletic girl with flowing blonde hair and a figure and legs that drew admiring glances from any males around. She had flown in from Sydney two days ago. This was to be a holiday break. At university she was studying business. It had been interesting at first but latterly she had become bored. However she felt she had done well enough in her practice exams to collect a second class. Dave's new English wife, Josie was staying at her parents' Auckland house. She wasn't quite sure why. Apparently Dave was still in England on some high-secret assignment and would be flying out later. Maggie liked Josie in spite of the girl's English accent. Josie looked very like her but as she was married and expecting she wouldn't be a rival with the boys.

Well, she'd got her Honda car back again. Josie had been driving it around town but had left it in perfect condition with a full gas tank. Maggie to her Honda and drove out of the city towards her boyfriend's family farm.

Robbie was a fellow student although he was studying medicine. During this vacation he would be needed on the farm. He didn't mind this, but in spite of his family's wish he would not become a farmer. She was on the road a short distance south of Manurewa when it happened. A farm tractor and a load of hay were stuck firmly across the road. Maggie stopped as she had no choice and she was irritated. She could see no one in the tractor cab nor anyone else on the roadside. She waited for three minutes and then blew a blast on her car horn. A car was coming up behind her and that, too, was forced to stop a metre from her rear bumper. Now she was alarmed. Men dressed in black with hoods appeared running, down the road from the direction of the stranded tractor. Who in hell were these…Now they had reached the car, three of them. Her door was wrenched open and she screamed. She was baffled and she was scared stiff. A rough gloved hand pushed her head back and a pair of dark eyes stared her in the face through tiny slits in the full face hood.

'Come on, darlin'. Nobody's goin' to hurt you, but you're coming along o' us.'

Maggie opened her mouth and sank her teeth into the offending glove. The man swore as he pulled his hand away.

'Don't do that, little girl,' said a second voice. 'You're coming with us. Nobody's going to hurt you, but your bloke will have to back off with his prying into what doesn't concern him.'

Maggie was forcibly dragged from the car and walked the short distance to the other motor, a modern jet black Audi. Into the rear seat she was pushed. A hypodermic needle was thrust into her bare arm and she knew nothing more.

Emily was feeling relaxed and happy. Her initial pregnancy test had now been confirmed positive. She would have to be careful, no alcohol for a start. And, much more important, any doubts her husband Tom had harboured had vanished. She knew that he was excited and it was genuine. Today she had a case to defend in Reading. With a bit of luck she could be home in time to have a meal out with the two men. Lily was happy to be looking after Peter for them. It seemed that in spite of the appalling cold weather life was good.

Tom was at home in his tiny office room catching up on paper work, or in reality dozens of emails and work on computer spread sheets. Dave had driven off in Josie's car. Was he getting anywhere with this murder puzzle? Dave wouldn't say. Dave and Josie were their friends and very close friends now and Josie had been alarmed by the attack on Dave on the road no more than a mile or so from their house. But Dave was a journalist. She herself had been a press victim when the truth of the Ollavasen murder had become public. She had been forced to hide in her house and not answer the phone for a whole week before the frenzy was diverted to some fresh sensation. Well, now the office phone was ringing and she heard Tom pick it up.

'What,' he shouted. 'Say that again!' Then she heard him slam the receiver down.

'Em,' he called. 'Come and listen to this. If it's genuine, I don't like it.'

Emily ran into the office. Tom turned to face her with an expression of real alarm.

'Listen to this. Oh, God I must ring Dave at once.' He pressed the replay button.

'Mr Manning. You're asking too many questions and asking things that are none of your business. Stop it. We're holding your girl in New Zealand. You see we're everywhere...'

Emily was shocked. The recorded voice was disembodied and metallic-obviously the work of some distorting system.

'I'll ring Dave now,' said Tom. 'He'll have to leave this business to the police.'

'He'll have to check if this is true.' Emily was really worried now. 'He sent Josie to New Zealand to protect her.'

'I know; if this is true then these people are very powerful. Quiet a minute and I'll ring Dave now.' He turned to face her again and his expression was grim.

CHAPTER 26

Dave had rung the Banner crime desk from his mobile. 'Can you research something for me?'

'Do my best,' replied the crime chief,

'I've a name: Paul Ferresier.' He spelt it phonetically.

'Yes ,got that. Is this connected with the Jebbs lynching?'

'It could be.'

'OK, I'll get back to you when we've checked.'

Dave put the phone back in his pocket and then it rang again. The caller was Tom Stoneman and a horrified Dave turned the car around and headed back to the cottage.

Tom and Emily both looked white faced and shocked. They played the threatening tape and Dave took in the full horror of the words. The metallic disguised voice only made the threats worse. 'Tom. I must ring Auckland. It'll be the middle of the night, but I must ring them.' He struggled to restrain the panic in his voice.

'Try Josie's mobile first,' Emily suggested.

'Yes, good shout.'

Following an agonising thirty seconds a very sleepy voice answered. 'I thought I'd turned this bloody thing off. Hey, is that you, Dave?'

'Josie, thank God. Just tell me are you all right?'

'Yes, I'm fine. I'm trying to catch some sleep. What's up?'

'Where are you?'

'Where do you think? I'm in Parnell at your people's house.'

'Josie, listen to me. I think you could be in danger. We've just had a threatening message and whoever sent it knows where you are. Go to the police and I'll relay them a copy of the message we've had.'

Josie sounded unconvinced. 'What's in this so called message?'

'Josie, you must take this seriously. I'm going to fly out and join you as soon as I can but in the meantime be careful. Tell my Dad and tell him to go to the police.'

'All right, if you say so. What's this message actually say?'

'That's the thing that's wound us all up. It says they've kidnapped you.'

'Well, they haven't yet. If we go to the police they'll want this message.'

'I know that. I'm going to send it by email attachment and I'll ring a copper I know right now. But I want you and Dad to go to the police first thing.'

'It'll have to be with your Dad anyway. Maggie's home and she's taken the car.'

Dave put the phone back and gave the others a wan smile. 'Well, she's fine now.'

'She sounded her usual self from what I could hear,' said Tom.

'I still don't like it. I'm going to ring Auckland. Emily, you and I have an old friend in the cops there.'

'Eh?'

'That's right. Inspector Le Bois.'

Emily stiffened in shock. 'What the hell?'

'No, not the mad one, but the son of. Don't you remember? He met you on the waterfront that time when you were slanging off your girlie enemies.'

'Oh, I remember, but he was nice, nothing like the other two with that name.' Emily remembered the young Auckland policeman who, it turned out, was the son of the obsessive madman who had died horribly within yards of her on that terrible morning in Surrey.

'You going to ring him now?' asked Tom. 'New Zealand is thirteen hours ahead of us in time. He'll be tucked up in bed with a tasty bimbo probably.'

Dave checked his watch. 'It'll be around one-thirty. That's not late by NZ standards. Anyway, he could be on duty.' He checked the data lists on his phone screen and wrote down two numbers. He took the mainline phone and dialled the first.

'Ah, Mick , good copper; thank God you're there.' Dave quickly told his listener about the message.

He stiffened again in real shock. 'Oh, bloody hell, man. They've snatched the wrong girl.'

Maggie was awake again. She felt as she had done many times after a big booze bash at uni. Her head ached and she felt mildly sick. But this time she knew something was different: something was wrong. She lay on a soft bed in a room where the bright light shone in through an open window. She turned away – it hurt her eyes. Where the hell was she? Now it was coming back: the jumbled memories; the car on the road to Robbie's farm. Men had grabbed her. Oh God, had she been raped? She felt around her body for cuts and bruises, but all seemed normal. But why her? This was Auckland, New Zealand;

snatching girls off the street might happen in Sydney or London but not here. She shut her eyes as she felt the tears begin to flow. Now she lapsed back into a semi-dream. She was sailing on the warm waters of the harbour in a little dinghy with her brother at the helm.

Dave replaced the phone. His face was strained and he looked ill. 'Oh God, no one knows where she is. The police haven't a clue. You see, this sort of thing doesn't happen there. Mike Le Bois says the last time they had a kidnap was some sort of feud in the Melanesian community. I've put it on the line. They're to find my sister and in the meantime they put a round the clock watch on Josie.'

'How on earth did these people come to grab the wrong girl?' asked Tom.

Emily caught him by the arm and glared. 'Tom, that's not tactful.'

'No, that's all right, Tom,' said Dave. 'I've been asking myself that and the police have no idea. I'll have to fly out ASAP. I'll contact the Banner and see if they can get me a priority flight.'

'Won't that make things worse?' Joe Manning had never felt like this before. His lovely daughter was a captive in the hands of God knew what band of desperadoes.

'We'll get these people, don't worry,' said the copper. 'We don't allow this sort of thing in our country.'

'But man, have they issued an ultimatum. What do they want – money?'

'As far as we can tell they want your son to stop asking questions about that multiple murder in England. I think if he makes a public declaration that might help.'

'But what's that got to do with our Margaret?'

'Our speculation is that they mistook her for your daughter-in-law: Mrs Josephine Manning. That's why we would like her to be with us when we give the news conference.'

Joe Manning was even more worried. 'But I said, won't that make things worse? What if they decide Maggie is superfluous…'

'No, Mr Manning. We don't think they would hurt her. They've got the wrong girl – understood. But if they hurt her they'll go down for a ten times longer stretch in clink. We're dealing with professionals here and they'll know that.'

Joe was still far from satisfied. 'What if they hold onto Maggie and come and get Josie? Then they'll have double hold on poor David.'

'We shall be putting a round the clock watch on Josephine. She's not to leave your house under any pretext. We'll judge the situation, but we may need to move her to a secure place of safety.'

'I guess you're right. But please be careful. We love our daughter more than anything in the world, but we love Josie too. She's a great girl.'

'I know, Please leave this to us. We will watch out for you and if these criminals try anything we'll get'em.'

Mike Le Bois said farewell to the distraught father and returned to his office. The man was telling the truth; no doubt whatever. Mike speculated that his own late demented father would probably have dreamed up some conspiracy and believed the aggrieved family were guilty themselves. He wondered, just wondered. Could he, Inspector Mike Le Bois, solve this one and with it catch the English multi-murder gang. How many promotions would that secure? David Manning was a nosy journo, but he did have a knack of finding out things that the slow Brit coppers missed. He understood that Dave was flying home and then they could have a share of ideas.

103

CHAPTER 27

Three days later Dave was on an airliner for New Zealand. The Daily Banner had come good with a last minute flight ticket on an aircraft with a political delegation. Dave was anxious, he could hardly think, let alone sleep. He was beset with anxiety and blaming himself for his impetuous investigation. He had somehow to hide his feelings from the surrounding politicians. They were hardly the sort of travelling company he would seek for preference and, as a journalist, they would be equally suspicious. In reality they were too involved in their own petty squabbles to take much notice of him.

Eventually they arrived at Auckland International Airport and, after an irritating pass through customs, he was free to find a taxi and take the trip into town to Parnell. He found this trip even worse than the long run in the airliner. Everywhere they passed familiar streets and buildings that he remembered from childhood. He could never have imagined his home city as a background for abduction and threats. At Parnell he found his family home with two police cars parked in the road and a policeman stood by the front door.

He showed his passport and ID to this officer and was allowed in. Josie ran across the hall and flung her arms around him sobbing into his shirt front. He kissed her and then gently led her to an armchair. 'Are you all right? Is the …the…'

Now she smiled through her tears. 'The baby is fine. The doctor checked me yesterday.'

'Thank God for that. What news of Maggie?'

Josie shook her head. 'We've no idea. She went out in her car to go to her boyfriend and she never got there. Then we also got that awful phone message that you got and then they found Maggie's car.'

Dave wasn't sure. 'Why on earth did they think she was you?'

'Yes, I've really worried about that. I blame myself. You see Maggie was away at university and I was driving her car. So someone saw me and got it wrong.'

Dave found this difficult to accept. New Zealand was a small tight-knit society. Even in this big city everyone knew everyone and his dad Joe was a leading lawyer. No, somebody who wasn't from around here had seen Josie in that battered old car and made the wrong connection.

'Josie, I've got a friend who's a top cop: he's working on this, but can you recall exactly every trip you made in that car? Where you went where you stopped? Anything about these trips, however trivial.'

'I didn't use it much. You see I don't know this town, but I used it to fetch the tins of varnish you wanted.'

'Tom,' called Emily. 'Just had an email. Dave's arrived in Auckland and Josie's safe. The police are guarding her.'

'That's a relief,' replied Tom. 'What about his sister?' Tom had just come in from work and was discarding his heavy anorak. It was still bitterly cold with a grey lowering sky and a threat of more snow.

'That's the worry. No one has any idea who it is that's got her or where she is.'

'Can't understand why they thought the girl was Josie. She three years younger and yes, they do look a bit alike, but not that much.'

Emily remembered the girl Maggie from the Auckland wedding. She was a pretty girl but a bit of a chatterbox. They had laughed at this as it fitted the alleged New Zealand stereotype of strong silent males, balanced by their shrill chattering womenfolk.

'So, Dave's out of action. It's all down to the police.' Tom frowned. 'We can't let Lorraine down. How say we go and see her and the kids again.'

'Yes, I think we should.'

'Lorri, how are you now?' Emily asked.

Lorraine smiled. 'I'm beginning to come to terms with it, but the kids are missing their dad every day.'

'Is there anything we can do?'

'No, not now; give it time and I'll be alright.' Lorraine rose to her feet and turned up the thermostat. 'That's better, it's colder than ever, but it's Dad who pays the heating bill.' She turned back to Emily. 'Where's Dave today?'

'He flew back to New Zealand yesterday, there's some family trouble.'

Tom had come back into the room. 'Tom,' asked Lorraine. 'Dave's been asking questions about Wally. Do you know if he's found anything?'

'Can't say for certain,' replied Tom. 'But there's some horrible big conspiracy around this and there's powerful people involved.'

'We know that – too right. Wally suspected something. You see he fixed it to go on that prison van because, and I'm only guessing, but I think he thought Jones was in some plot to spring Jebbs.'

Yes, thought Tom; but not to spring him but to hang him. But there must have been some bigger motive. Did Jebbs and Jones know something that would embarrass these millionaires?

All the nightmare they were going through hadn't stopped Josie from being curious. She was in her husband's home country, but she was surprised and pleased how much was similar to Britain. The police had almost identical uniforms to the coppers back home although the sergeant in charge wore his three stripes upside down American style. She liked Chief Inspector Le Bois. He seemed wholly different to everything she had been told about the man's father. That man had been the mad Sussex copper who had followed a false trail when Emily had been abducted and paid with his life: shot by the SAS as Emily fled.

The Inspector began his interview. 'Mrs Manning, may I call you Josie?'

'Of course, I'd like that.'

'Good, we're not that formal here. Now can you recall everywhere you went in that Honda?'

'Well, sort of. Let me trace it for you on the street map. You see I was on my way to the yacht chandlers but I did lose my way and the car doesn't have a satnav.'

Josie stared at the street map but was not much wiser. 'I crossed a road bridge and I knew I was in the wrong place. I asked in a shop and they told me I was in... They told me this was Chelsea, but it doesn't look much like the one back home.'

The Inspector laughed. 'No big soccer team around there. They do play the real game though.'

'Rugby?'

'Of course – what else?'

'All right. Do you remember the name of the shop?'

'Yes it was a Qualistore twenty four-hour.'

The Inspector wrote a note. 'We'll check it out. What did you do then?'

'I turned around and re-crossed that bridge. Another ten minutes and I found the right road and came to the Yachtiegear store. I bought the varnish tins and came back here.'

'Any more wrong turns?'

'No, the road signs to here are really good. Better than in London.'

'Well, that's good to hear.'

'Inspector, can you tell me anything. Is there any sign of Maggie? I feel awful about this. It seems they thought she was me.'

'Be assured we are following all lines of enquiry towards a satisfactory resolution.'

Josie couldn't help it. Despite everything she giggled. 'Oh Inspector you're talking British copspeak.'

Maggie screwed her eyes shut against the sunlight that poured through an unclean window glass. She wasn't at home but where was she? And what had happened? Hadn't she been driving in her car on the way to see… Oh, yes she remembered a tractor across the road and horrible masked men. She'd been abducted, but why…why? Why for Christ's sake pick on her? She was no one – just a student. Was it rape? In sick fear she tried to sit up. She could feel no pain or bruises, but what would she feel? She felt sick and she had a pounding headache. She tried to focus on her surroundings. She was lying on a crude metal framed single bedstead, the sort of thing the military slept on. The room was nothing; just a square gloomy box with a shabby door and the same dirty window. The air had a pervading smell. It was not unpleasant but it was oddly familiar. Somewhere, not far away, she could hear a motorbike engine or was it? No, she knew that sound. It was a two-stroke boat outboard motor. So she must be somewhere near the water. It was no good she felt sick and giddy and she fell back on the bed and once again lapsed in a world of nightmare.

She awoke, she never knew how much later, but the sunshine was not so bright and no longer beaming through the window. She stiffened with fright. A man was in the room staring at her. He was really scary: large, fat and bald, dressed in jeans and a sleeveless T-shirt. Now her eyes were focussing better and she could see his arms were heavily tattooed with flowers and a funny military style badge. And his neck was encircled by a tattooed snake. 'Hello, you awake, sweetheart?'

Maggie was scared but determined not to show it. 'Who are you and why am I here?'

'All right, Josephine, you've nothing to worry about. You'll be safe if you do what you're told.'

'What did you call me? My name's Margaret.'

'No, that won't wash, love. I'm going now. Bring you some food later.'

'Can't I have a drink of water? I am so thirsty.'

The sullen face suddenly had a ghost of a smile. 'All right. See what I can do.'

It was true, she was in desperate thirst, but the headache was lessening. Why had he called her Josephine? Napoleon's wife was called that. Maggie had this odd memory of history at school. But the fat guy was a Brit, a Pom and newly arrived by the way he talked. Josephine, Jo, oh God, Josie, that was it; how stupid they must be to think she's Dave's Josie. But why – everyone in Auckland knew her family. Dad was an important figure and the whole family had featured in that TV programme last year and the TV had featured Dave and Josie's wedding. Why on earth mistake her for Josie. Josie was a few years older and they didn't look that much alike; even different hair colour.

'Darling, can you remember anyone you spoke to?' Dave cradled his wife in his arms.

'I was in this area called Chelsea,' she replied. 'And I asked the way in a Qualistores shop. It was one of those quick-serve open twenty four hour places. You know, we've got them in the UK. The girl at the checkout told me to go back across the bridge. I did that and, blow me, there was the Yachtiegear store that I'd missed.'

'Can you describe the checkout girl?'

'Not sure. I didn't take much notice but she was young – bit older than teens and looked a bit like Chloe.'

'OK, she's probably Polynesian, but that doesn't man a thing these days. No, what do you remember about Yachtiegear?'

'Well, it wasn't much different to a boat store back home. They were helpful and found what I wanted, but yes, the guy who loaded the car was a Brit. Definitely spoke with a London accent.'

'Could you describe him?'

'He was ugly, bald with loads of tattoos.'

Emily picked up the ringing telephone. 'Can I speak to David Manning?' The voice was cultivated and female.

Emily was puzzled. 'I'm afraid he isn't here any more. He's in New Zealand.'

'Oh,' the voice sounded upset. 'I've tried ringing his mobile number. But he gave me your number as well, but only for emergency.'

Emily's lawyer tone was emerging. 'Would you be so kind as to tell me who you are?'

108

'Oh, I'm sorry. My name is Jasmine Harris-Evans.' The voice faltered. 'Mr Manning spoke to my sister the other day. Are you Mrs Stoneman?'

'Correct.'

'Oh, I'm so sorry to have troubled you, but Mr Manning, David that is, asked my sister to contact him if I was worried.'

'May I ask what it is that's worrying you and may we know the name of your sister?'

'Did Dave tell you anything about the questions he's asking?'

Emily was beginning to be annoyed. It should be her asking the questions. 'David is a journalist. I think you should be talking to him.'

'Oh no, he told me and my sister that he'd spoken to you about the murders. He said one of your friends had lost her husband.'

'Are you referring to Lorraine Markham?'

'Yes, I think so, but I don't know her.'

Emily was even more irritated now. 'Before we take this further, may I ask who this sister of yours is?'

'Oh, I'm sorry. I thought you knew. Cerise, she's a widow now but her husband was Graham Blake-Grass.'

In spite of everything Emily was intrigued now. 'Oh yes, my father met Mrs Blake-Grass at a reception on his yacht, Mr Blake-Grass's yacht that is. It wasn't long before he died. But he said Mrs Blake-Grass was worried about something. You see my Dad is the sort of person people want to pour out their troubles to.'

'Perhaps we should talk to you. I'm told you are a lawyer.'

'No, if you've discovered anything compromising you must go to the police.'

'I know, we will, but Cerise is frightened. The police tried to accuse her of Graham's murder, but that's rubbish; she adored him.'

'I think you will find that the police are fair and they will listen.'

'Yes, we will talk to them but please, could we confide in you first and then maybe you can find and talk to David.'

Dave stood and sized up the front of Yachtiegear Auckland. It was an impressive showroom that had once been a harbourside restaurant. The restaurant had fallen on hard times and Yachtiegear had snapped up the site. Dave smiled. This had been a vegetarian restaurant, with a loyal following, but definitely not in tune with mainstream meat eating culture. He picked up his briefcase and strolled through the automatic doors. The store was no different to its equivalents in the UK, Australia or anywhere where boats were sailed. The shelves bulged with yacht fittings, compasses, books and charts. The atmosphere had a delicious scent of paint and rope that made him itch to be back afloat. He fingered the little black radio alarm in his top pocket.

The pay checkout was manned by a pretty little mixed race girl. 'Anything I can show you?' she asked.

'I need some anti-foul and ten metres of halyard line.'

The girl pointed him to the relevant shelves. Dave returned with four heavy tins and a full drum of line. 'Bit heavy these. Is anyone around who can help me load?'

'Yeah, Paul's in the office. I'll get 'im.'

The man who came was burly, bald and had a snake tattoo around his neck. Dave gave him one look and pressed the alarm button. Within seconds the police had surged into the shop. The bald man had foolishly picked up a boat paddle and was waving it menacingly.

As the police began to spread out through the shop their leader confronted the man.

'Chief Inspector Le Bois,' He waved a warrant card and a sheet of paper. 'I have here a warrant to search these premises. I would advise you to put that bit of wood down and not resist further.'

Two policeman ran up a steep metal stairway. Seconds later came the sounds of splintering wood and a squeal of alarm. The men emerged at the head of the stairs and with them was a girl, his sister.

'Maggie,' he cried out in relief.

She tripped carefully down the metals stairs and flung her arms around him. 'Oh, Dave, how did you know I was here?' she was sobbing into his shirtfront now. 'I thought you were overseas.'

CHAPTER 28

'What are you going to do now, boy?' asked Dave's father.

Dave was feeling subdued and he didn't need this interrogation. 'I'm going to stay here with Josie and you for the next week or so anyway. Inspector Le Bois is questioning the arrested men and I need to hear what comes out of this.'

'We don't think you should be meddling with this business. Cripes sake, Dave, you're a sports writer, not a detective.'

'Of course I am, but one of the men murdered in England was our friend. I'm not trying to solve the puzzle. I'm only after evidence connected with sailing. And the people who took Maggie are connected with the main suspects.'

'What do you say girls?' Joe addressed his wife Helen and Maggie and Josie.

'We've got to help this investigation and the one in England,' said Josie.

Maggie suddenly looked angry and her words were unexpected. 'No, Dad, Dave has got to carry on. I want the truth and anyway, do we allow these new arrived Poms to snatch girls off the street?'

'Right,' said Emily. 'You, Cerise, are pretty certain that Jebbs was a blackmailer and that he had some hold over your late husband.'

Cerise winced and glanced at her sister. 'I think so, but I don't know what it was about and it doesn't mean Graham had Jebbs killed.'

'No, I accept that, but someone wanted Jebbs out of the way. I doubt the lynching was for revenge only.'

Tom intervened. 'But would anyone want to kill the man simply because he filmed them doing what comes naturally?'

'I agree,' said Emily. 'One would assume it was something more serious than that.'

She turned to Jasmine. 'The email refers to Iver, but your husband's name is Ifor and we don't know who Paul F is. I expect the police have traced the email address by now but they're not likely to tell us.' Emily looked at her husband. 'Hello, Tom, what's up?'

'It can't be,' Tom looked puzzled. 'I know a man we called Iver but that was a joke. He isn't Welsh and that's not his name. But, no it can't be him, He's a clever guy but harmless.'

'Who are you talking about?' asked Emily.

'Oh, never mind. It's rubbish anyway. It just rang a chord so to speak.'

'Can we have a name?'

'No, I'd rather pass on that one. It would be downright libellous if I was wrong.'

Emily smiled, 'I think you mean slander.'

'There speaks the lawyer.'

Emily looked at the guests. 'Any idea who Paul F is? What was Amanda Furness's husband called?'

Jasmine frowned. 'It was all over the papers at the time but I don't think he's a Paul. He would have good reason to kill Jebbs, but the papers say he's a university lecturer. I doubt he has the means to mount a lynching.'

Emily continued. 'When Jebbs killed his ex-wife he killed five other people. They were just names in the papers at the time but do we know anything more?'

'One was a Tory politician: a Ms Hopeson,' said Jasmine.

'No tears for her then,' replied Emily.

Tom laughed. 'Ignore her; she's a bloody Lib Dem.'

'Oh no, we'll just ignore you,' Emily grinned.

'Regardless of politics it seems she wasn't very nice,' said Cerise. 'Her husband was given care of their child so in spite she cut him out of their business.'

'Do we know this for certain?'

'Yes, the papers were full of it.'

'Do we know anything about the other four who died?'

'They were all female but one of the others was a vicar from that village.'

'No tears there then,' said Tom.

This time Emily glowered at him. 'Do you have to display this misogyny in front of our guests? I'm sure her congregation were very distressed and rightly so,' she turned to the others. 'Ignore him this time. He's only trying to wind us all up.'

Inspector Le Bois stared at his suspect. 'Mr Ferresier, we have generously allowed you to stay in our country for six months and we've even given you a work permit and allowed you to drive our streets. Now you repay us by abducting a young lady who is a citizen of our nation and well liked. Have you an explanation?'

'She was in danger,' Ferresier replied.

'Yes, from you and whoever employs you.'

The burly looking prisoner made no reply, but looked even more surly as sweat ran down his face and over the tattoos on his neck. 'No comment.'

'Very well, if you want to be like that. You're remanded in custody. Take him away and I'll talk to the girl.' Ferresier was removed, muttering threats.

Next, the woman constable brought in the female branch manager. She was named as Penelope Maria Rakurua. Around thirty, mixed race, Le Bois assumed, and genuinely scared. He would be gentle this time and hopefully learn something.

'Right, may I call you Penelope?' he smiled reassuringly.

Some of the fear receded in her expression. 'I'm Penny to most people.'

'Penny. Police in England have passed me an email you sent. Here, it reads: *We've put your Poms to work on light duties and driving. They know fuck all about boats.*

'Do you agree you mailed that? It's in your name.'

'Yeah, those blokes were sent by our head office in England. Someone fiddled them work permits for here. But as I said, they didn't know bow from stern or port from starboard.'

Le Bois smiled. 'And obviously you do.'

'Oh yeah. I've messed around wi' boats all my life – love'em.'

'You worked in this store before the present owners took it over?'

'That's right, I've worked here since I was sixteen. It was the Waterfront restaurant then, bit o' a dump. I waited on table. Then it became a yacht shop but didn't do much, Yachtiegear may be a Brit concern but they've done us good. Trade's picked up no end.'

Le Bois now turned on his severe expression. 'You realise now that these two characters were, it seems, involved in abducting this girl. How much do you know about it?'

'They threatened me. The told me they had something valuable stored in the room and if I went near it they'd take it out on my little girl,' She was sobbing now. 'Katie's only two. My man's pissed off and we're all on our own.'

'That's doubly serious. Didn't it occur to you to tell us about it?'

Penny was weeping with no restraint and she was genuine; no act. 'I was scared and I didn't know if you would believe me. Those blokes have got the man in England behind them and he carries a lot of clout.'

113

'Can you remember this Englishman's name?'

'Yes, I've got it here somewhere, but the one I talked to isn't the one who is the Yachtiegear big boss. May I look in the office? It'll be on my computer.'

Penny left the room with the police woman and returned a few minutes later. She handed Le Bois an email print out. 'I dunno' who that bloke is but he says he speaking on the orders of Ifor the big boss man.'

'So you've never met this bloke?'

'No, never heard of him – funny name he's got. But we know Ifor. He flew out here six months ago and we liked him. All we girls fancied him and he got off wi' a couple o' them. Tell me; was the little girlie locked up in here being kept for him?'

Le Bois grinned. 'Now then, Penny. It's me that's asking the questions. OK, you can go now. Your shop is closed for the next day or so while we investigate, but anything you recall that might help us you must say.'

A very relieved Penny scuttled out of the room. 'Right, bring in the other Pom.'

'Josie, I want you to stay here and take care of yourself and the baby. Nothing else matters. Once I'm back in England I'll keep in touch.'

Josie hung onto him her arms around his neck. 'You will be careful. If these people can't get at me they'll go for you.'

'Darling, I will be more than careful. I will let the world know I'm not prying into the Jebbs affair any more. Then hopefully they'll leave me in peace.'

'But you will keep listening. We owe Lorraine that at least.'

'Oh, yes, but I promise I will be subtle.'

Dave felt torn in two. His journalist's instinct drove him to pursue this story to the bitter end. But he owed it to Josie and his own people not to do anything stupid. If his opponents were all like the fat bastard he encountered on the road that day then he wasn't worried. At that moment his phone rang.

'Ken here, from the Banner. Hope I haven't caught you at wrong time of day.'

'No, Ken. It's just ten p.m. here and tomorrow I fly back to the UK. What have you got for me?'

'Interesting but maybe not that relevant but that Gloria Hopeson the woman Jebbs shot, well her dad was Ferdy Modlington the dirty old lord. She was the Honourable Gloria Modlington but she married a guy called Hopeson and he does have connections with the boat business.'

'All right, Ken, don't keep me in suspense.'

'Hopeson was cut out of his ex-wife's haulage firm business, but it seems he was already one of your yachties. He's got a salesman's job working for Magnum Millennium Marine. Not a bad number. He's in Dubai at the moment selling boats. As I say not a bad little number, eh?'

'You know that Blake-Grass owned Magnum Millennium?'

'Well he's dead. But now I gather Hopeson's got a cousin that works for them and he pulled a few favours.'

'I know hardly anything about Magnum, would I know this cousin?'

'He's their chief designer, name of Pollingham...' There was a pause. 'Dave, Ferdy Modlington says he was set up and he doesn't live too far away from where your friends are in Hampshire. He won't talk to the Banner but when we mentioned you he said fine – he'll meet you.'

'Yes, Ken that's all very well but it's not connected with the story I'm following is it?'

'Well you can judge that yourself; but old Ferdy says he was set up by Jones.'

By the time that Dave reached Heathrow he was tired, disconnected and far from looking forward to the tasks ahead. However he recovered Josie's Nissan and drove across London to Bayswater where he could be reunited with his own Renault. The weather was still bitterly cold, the more so after the Auckland sunshine. Dave understood that the main routes to the south and west were now clear and running smoothly. He would spend a lonely night in the flat and then head for Hampshire in the morning.

He thought hard about the task ahead. For Josie's sake he would not make it too obvious that he was continuing to follow the Jebbs murder trail. Old Ferdy Modlington lived in a Berkshire village called Huntbourne a little bit north of the border with Hampshire. There was a limit as to how long he would impose on his friends Emily and Tom. He only hoped he could produce a result and forget the whole bloody business.

Dave finally reached Emily and Tom's house in mid-afternoon. Emily was in Reading on a court brief but Tom was at home with Peter and Lily.

'Tom,' Dave asked. 'Have you ever come across a guy called Hopeson in the big yacht business?'

'How big?'

'Well he works for Magnum-Millennium.'

'Christ, that's mega bucks – not really my scene.'

'Well, he's also Ferdy Modlington's son-in-law.'

Tom bristled. 'Not that nasty little perv. Em sorted that one out in court.'

'Well, I've got to talk to him on behalf of the Banner…'

'Don't envy you that.'

'But listen, Tom. It seems there could be a link to the Jebbs case.'

'You think so. Well, don't push it too hard. By the way, the police have finally released poor Wally's body; funeral's in two day's time.'

CHAPTER 29

Ferdy Modlington lived in *The Georgian House*. Dave found this was not a stately home but a rather nice detached building in the village main street. He discovered this only after he'd asked for directions in the village shop. Here he had a surprise. The villagers were not hostile to their titled neighbour. They seemed to agree that he had become the victim of a scam. Dave was regarded with some suspicion until he claimed to be a relative from New Zealand on a short visit. He had an appointment with the lord at two- thirty which left him time for a bite to eat at the local pub. Then, leaving his car in the pub's parking lot, he walked to the said *Georgian House.*

No butler answered the door nor housemaid, but an elderly lady dressed in a lurid red gown. 'You must be Mr Manning,' she greeted him. 'Ferdy will be so glad you've come,' she dropped her voice to a whisper. 'He's got lots to get off his chest.'

'Hey there. Is that the journalist fellow? Show him in here.' A deep aristocratic voice boomed from nearby. 'Lizzie, bring him in the study and then get us a cup of coffee. A short round stature round faced man had appeared driving an electric wheelchair. Dave had seen pictures of Modlington in his political days but these had shown a younger man with a full head of dark hair. 'Mr Manning, I wouldn't normally welcome a journo in this house, but I've read your articles in *World Yachting* and other papers and I like your style. If some of your colleagues have an ear for scandal, as I understand it you have in interest in truth.'

'I try my best but really I'm a sports writer. I was dragged into that business last year because it involved sailing.'

The man thrust out a hand. 'I'm so sorry I should have said. I'm Modlington and this is my dear wife Elizabeth. Lizzie is making coffee but would you like something stronger on this cold morning?'

'No thanks, I'm driving.'

'Very well, now into my study and down to business.'

Dave followed the little man into a nicely furnished study. A log fire was burning in one corner and opposite was a fine antique writing desk topped with a filing cabinet and a laptop computer. Landscape paintings hung on the walls as well as a large flat screen television.

'I expect you followed my court case,' Modlington began.

At this point Dave had to interrupt. 'Before we start I think I must tell you that Mrs Stoneman the prosecuting attorney is a close friend of my wife and I.'

Modlington smiled. 'I have no quarrel there. She was a pretty little thing and was only doing her best with the material the police provided. It was that material that was false and planted by the man Jones. I expect you've been told that Jebbs murdered my poor daughter.'

Dave nodded and hoped he looked suitably contrite. 'I know, you have our condolences.'

Modlington sighed. 'We miss her of course and cannot mourn the death of her killer. She was headstrong young thing and obsessively ambitious and she neglected our little granddaughter and treated her poor husband appallingly. But she was our little girl and we loved her dearly.'

Dave remained silent as he watched the grief on the other man's face. It was odd but Modlington did not fit Dave's preordained idea of a paedophile. He waited while the man recovered his poise.

'Jones?' said Dave.

Modlington, with an obvious effort, shook himself back to reality. 'Yes, I am, or was before this business, the patron of the Charity for Preserved Ships. We need to arouse interest in the younger generation so I devised a scheme where we show parties of school children around historic ships. The man Jebbs was known as a nautical photographer, so unfortunately, in retrospect we took him on to photograph these visits.'

'And Jones?'

'That is where my problems began. Jones told Jebbs he knew of a primary school near Bristol who would like a tour of the SS Great Britain. The tour took place and Jebbs took the pictures. But Jebbs came to me and told me that three of these youngsters had told him they were being sexually abused by Jones. You see, Jones was stupid enough to come on that tour with Jebbs. Then Jebbs found out that Jones was supplying these same children to the paedophile prison.'

'Did Jones admit that?'

'No, these three little ones told Jebbs, and he wanted to take them straight to the police. But the kids were scared of the police. Seems they were from poor backgrounds and a charity sponsored them for their own school.

'One morning Jebbs brought Jones here and I confronted the scoundrel and told him I would use my influence to see him arrested and prosecuted.

'Then Jones became all smarmy and handed me what he said were discs with photographs of my children's ship visits. I told him I would proceed with handing him to the police. Jebbs removed Jones. I put the discs in a drawer and then I telephoned the police. They called and were less than helpful. Instead they seized Jones' photographic discs and twenty four hours later I was charged with being in possession of indecent photographs. Meanwhile that rat Jones went free.'

Dave was impressed now. Modlington was telling the truth, of that he was convinced. 'Please, the last thing I want to do is intrude on grief, but can you give me any reason why Jebbs should have gone mad and killed?'

'I understand that Jebbs had a burning grievance against his ex-wife. She, and another woman in that group, had connived with Jones in supplying victims for perverts.

My poor girl confronted him and tried to remove the gun. It seems the man had a wild look, and at that point was beyond reason. Jebbs told a prison warder that Jones trying to smear my honour was a final straw.'

'Please, would you know the name of that warder?'

'Yes, as it happens I asked. He was the same poor man, Markham, who was murdered along with Jones. I met him and he told me himself. Unfortunately he too was murdered so we couldn't call him as a witness.'

CHAPTER 30

It was still bitterly cold but at least the sun was shining. Inside the little Catholic church it was warmer and the pews were full of mourners. Dave, with Tom and Emily, sat near the middle of the congregation. Tom sat with a stoical expression, Emily was occasionally dabbing a handkerchief to her tears and Dave felt an emptiness that was wholly alien to his normal nature. He wished Josie could have been at his side. Around them sat a mixture of Wally's friends and work colleagues: the prison governor with his burly male and female prison staff, plus familiar faces from the sailing scene and others from Lorraine's Afro-Caribbean family and friends. Lorraine and her children had taken their places at the front and now the coffin was carried in by the four bearers. Dave noted it was not the pinewood box such as his old uncle had been buried in but a basket weave container topped by flowers and a wreath.

The service was mercifully a shortened version of the funeral mass. The address was given by the Vice-Commodore of the sailing club and was moving and struck exactly the right note. Now they were all outside as the coffin was placed gently in the hearse and with close family following departed for the crematorium. Lorraine had rushed over to them and kissed them all. She was tearful and stoical all in one. 'You must come to our wake party later on,' she said as her two children stood white faced and hunched against the cold wind.

The wake was not as dismal an affair as Dave had dreaded. It was held in a little upstairs restaurant in Gosport. The room was warm and although it was hardly a happy occasion the conversation was full of memories of Wally Markham. All three of them began to relax. Tom was first to sample the generous spread of food and first to grab his pint of beer.

'Dave,' asked Emily? 'Can you tell me what you made of Modlington?'

'Well, you won't like this…'

'You're going to tell me he was set up aren't you?'

'Yes, I'm sorry Em, but he convinced me.'

'Well, I'm not too put out. I had a few doubts, but when it came down to the trial it was the jury's decision.'

'Don't worry, he doesn't blame you – he made a point of saying so.'

Emily grimaced. 'A century ago innocent men went to the gallows. I couldn't have lived with that if I'd been prosecuting. Will he appeal?'

'He didn't say, but I hope the Banner will take up his case.'

Emily smiled now. 'Oh, come on Dave. They've already done all they can to blacken him.'

Dave was gazing out of a window. 'That office block over there; that's where Sam Pollingham works. I've been there. You know his cousin was involved in some of this. He could have a grievance.'

'Who is that?' asked Tom.

'He's Hopeson ex-husband of the girl that Jebbs murdered when she tried to get the gun off him.'

'And you say she was Modlington's daughter,' Emily sighed. 'This is getting far too complicated for me.'

'For me too,' said Dave.

'You'd be better off reporting on the rugby,' said Tom.

'You've said it, but I've got to keep listening. I owe that to Wally.'

'And to Lorraine,' said Emily.

Dave continued. 'Apparently this Hopeson works for Magnum selling yachts in Dubai.'

'Rich Arabs,' Tom replied. 'I thought they were all on the way out.'

'That's the dictators,' said Emily. 'The rich ones won't be parted from their cash that easily whatever regime takes over.'

Dave frowned. 'I don't really know Sam Pollingham that well. I don't move in his world. But I would like to know about this cousin.'

'Tell you what,' said Emily. 'I'll ask my dad. He's not a motor boat man but he does business with these sorts of people.'

'Not rich Arabs,' Tom smiled.

'I couldn't say, but he makes sails for the sort of people who know rich Arabs.'

'Can't help thinking the solution to all this lies with Jebbs.' Dave was feeling despondent as were both Emily and Tom. The funeral was some sort of closure but the felt desperately for Lorraine and her children.

'He must've been a psycho,' said Tom.

'That's what concerns me. The man commits a mass killing and that certainly looks like madness, but it seems Wally thought there was a plot to spring Jebbs on his way to court...'

'To spring him to kill him,' said Emily.

'Yes, but on the face of it the people behind that plot were sober prosperous citizens. Why did they want Jebbs suppressed? In other words, who was he and what hold did he have over all of them?'

'By them I assume you mean Blake-Grass.'

'Yes, I'm certain he was involved, but someone else wanted him out of the way as well. So if I can find out what Jebbs knew and who he knew we could be on our way to solving this and avenging poor Wally.'

Tom looked worried. 'Hold on a minute, Dave. You've been warned to keep out of this. Look what's just happened to Josie and your sister.'

'Oh, don't worry. I'm not going to prowl around shouting from the rooftops…'

In spite of everything Emily smiled. 'Oh, I like the analogy. Prowling around on rooftops sounds pretty dire; don't tell Health and Safety.' She paused looking serious now. 'I'll go and ring my Dad and ask him about Magnum boats and this Hopeson guy.'

Shortly afterwards they said farewell to poor Lorraine and to several of their sailing friends who were present and drove home to Alresford. Tom went into the kitchen and made them all a second cup of coffee. The world outside the cottage was still cold and the snow was beginning to have a look of permanency. When Emily returned from the study her face was alight with excitement. 'I got hold of Dad and believe it or not he knows Hopeson. He owns a thirty-footer and he's made sails for him. Dad likes him; says he seemed a decent guy and genuine sailor, and he paid on the nail – very straight. He's going to try and find some more detail for us.'

Dave had never felt so torn in two. The abduction of sister, Maggie had stunned and sickened him and the fact that the abductors had picked the wrong girl made little difference. He loved them both in different ways. The encounter with more villains on the road had not scared him. He knew he could have dealt with them there and then. The police were getting nowhere, or so it seemed, although they were hardly going to update him on their work. Nor had the Banner crime desk had any more luck. Certainly, following recent scandals, individual coppers no longer talked to the press about their findings. He was still being well paid although in the current cold freeze sport, Premier League apart, was mostly postponed. The Banner had told him he could report the big rugby game in Reading that Saturday, but they still wanted him to listen out in the case of the Sussex murders. His throwing doubt on the Modlington conviction had not been well received in the Banner office. A "dirty old lord" had been too good a story for them to backtrack on now. Nor could he drop his own investigation. Poor Wally's funeral and Lorraine's heartbreak had stiffened his resolve. He pulled out his mobile phone and rang to make an appointment.

'Hi, big daughter. Not in court today?' Kirsten greeted Emily. 'Why this surprise visit?'

Earlier that morning Emily had rung her parents' home and told them she was coming but without giving a reason.

'I'm not due in court until next Monday, but I need to talk to you both about a boat or rather the man who owns it.'

'Where's Peter?'

'Sorry, but I've left him with Lily. I didn't want him out in this cold.'

Kirsten turned and called Emily's father. He emerged slowly from his office supported by a walking stick. Emily explained that Dave was being cautious and could he tell them anything about the man Hopeson.

'He's always seemed a good guy to me and he's nice to do business with. I wish we had a few more like that.'

'He's a rather tragic figure,' said Kirsten. 'His wife was murdered being brave and trying to stop Jebbs from killing. But she had divorced him, don't know why, and then she threw him out of their haulage business. She divorced the husband and, I can't believe this but she asked for him to have custody of their little daughter. What sort of woman does that?'

'She was an obsessively ambitious politician,' Emily grunted.

'Yes,' said Steve. 'But he's rebuilt his life with Magnum and oddly enough it was Blake-Grass who rescued him. Seems he's a good salesman, but he's not really a motorboat man. He owns a rather nice Feltham Thirty-Two. We've made him two suits of sails.'

'Did you know he has a cousin in the yacht business?'

'No, should I?'

'He's Sam Pollingham who designs for Magnum.'

'Really, sleepy old Sam...'

Kirsten laughed. 'Who's talking about old? The man must be fifty at most.'

Steve grinned. 'Sam's a clever bloke – used to be a top rugby player. Does Dave Manning know that?'

'If it's rugby I expect he does.'

'Yes, Sam played a few times for one of the top London sides – can't remember which. But he was always a clever fellow. Got a master's degree in engineering design. He started in the Royal Navy constructors service.'

'What can you tell me about this Mr Hopeson?'

'Oh, Dennis? Yes, he had a raw deal from that ex-wife. It's sad that she died in that way but she was a tough nut. True, she was a politician, the Tory candidate for her area. From what Hopeson told us she was ruthlessly ambitious: passed the upbringing of her child to him. Brave lady though; plenty wouldn't have intervened with Jebbs.'

Emily wondered. Why? Who didn't want Jebbs to stand trial? The lynching didn't really make sense. Jebbs hanging had taken place miles away. Who among the lynch party had a personal motive? Or did Jebbs have some knowledge that would be embarrassing if he revealed it in court? If some wealthy conspiracy headed by the likes of Blake-Grass had planned this, then it seemed that had to be the likeliest reason. But what could a roving photographer like Jebbs have possibly known that was so embarrassing? Had he shot some discreet footage of B-G with one of his mistresses? No, she doubted that B-G would have given a damn however distressing for poor Cerise. It had to be something much more threatening. If Dave insisted on going on with his investigation then surely that was where he should look.

Dave reached the Magnum Millennium offices at eleven o'clock the next morning. He had an appointment arranged by phone the previous day. He was surprised to find Cerise Blake-Grass in the manager's office and with her was the man he wanted to see: Dennis Hopeson. He had also rung Cerise herself the previous evening. His excuse was that he wanted to meet Hopeson because he was interested in buying a Quantam yacht. Cerise had told him that Dennis was home from the Middle East and was temporarily occupying the chief executive's seat at Magnum. That was a big jump from salesman. Hopeson had certainly repaired his fortunes.

Dennis was an impressive man, in many ways the quintessential offshore yachtsman. He was slim, tanned, obviously fit and aged around forty, with a mop of curly fair hair. Dave had gathered that Modlington had liked his son-in-law. He wondered what had driven his ex-wife to kick him out. Possibly the ambitious politician had become a boat widow, or more than likely, the fit looking Hopeson had been cheating. And where was the little girl he'd been given in custody? Dave smiled inwardly. He was thinking like a Banner reporter.

Dave noted that Cerise looked less than grief stricken and far more relaxed than on their last encounter. She smiled at him and asked if he would like a cup of coffee. Dave smiled in return and accepted the offer. She tripped out of the room. Yes, that was the right term. Something had definitely happened, and her late husband was not yet in the grave.

'Right, Mr Manning. How can we help you?' Hopeson was leaning back in his padded chair and eying Dave with a knowing look. Well, here was an intelligent guy, not to be underrated.

'Steve Simpson, the sailmaker says you own a Feltham thirty-footer. It's a design that might suit me but I've never sailed on one.'

'Well I glad you are interested. I love my boat. She's a comfortable cruiser and a half-decent racer,' he paused. 'But, come on Mr Manning that's not why you're really here, is it?'

CHAPTER 31

'Mr Manning, Cerise here has already told me all about your investigations. I don't read the Daily Banner but I know you from the yachting press. You know my cousin Sam and I saw you at the funeral of poor Wallace.'

Dave felt his spirits sink. He was rumbled. 'You knew Wally Markham?'

'Yes, nice guy and good seaman – he crewed on my *Somerset Rose* in last year's Round the Island.' Hopeson stared at Dave, inscrutable, but at the same time not unfriendly. 'So David, may I call you David? And I'm Dennis. So, David you and I are, I think, on the same side.'

'Yes, I hope we are. I'm not stirring trouble to please the Daily Banner, but Wally and Lorraine were friends of my wife and myself and friends with many of our friends. I'm only looking out for information relevant to the world of sailing. I want the people who killed my friend and your wife caught and dealt with.'

'Well, I'm sorry about Gloria's death and she was a brave girl in the way she died. But she and I were a total mismatch...'

Cerise had re-entered the office with a tray of cups and a coffee pot. She placed the tray on the desk and stood behind Dennis with both hands on his shoulders. Yes, thought Dave. Perhaps her sister Jasmine was right. Cerise needed to move on and she had found another dominant male to cling to.

Dave stared back. 'Jebbs was unbalanced and a bit of a hypocrite regarding religion and Jones was a total scoundrel. Please, can you tell me what was the hold that Jebbs had over Blake-Grass and why did Jones get away with what he did for so long?'

'Hmm, Jebbs and religion,' said Hopeson. 'My family come from Scotland. Historically our favourite son, Robbie Burns, was a devout Presbyterian but he still managed I don't know how many mistresses and love children.'

'I think I can give you a hint as to where Jebbs was digging,' said Cerise. 'I think it had to do with Graham's business dealings in South America. There's a man who lives somewhere up Petersfield way...'

'He's not called Garcia?' Dave asked.

'No, he's got a Spanish sort of name but not that.'

'Sorry, I didn't mean to interrupt. Go on.'

'I don't know the exact name but it sounded like Romeo. I overhead Graham on the phone one day and afterwards I checked to see who he had been calling. Luckily he never found out I'd done that. I didn't really take in the name but I expect it's on the record still.

'Anyway, Graham was angry, but then he always was. But this time I guess he was worried. He was telling the man that...let me recall exactly, yes he said: "It's been a very good return on our investment but I don't like the unethical element. I could be in deep shit if any do-gooders found out..."'

Dave was intrigued. 'I know your late husband had interests in Chile and Argentina. My newspaper says he had money invested in Olifa on the west coast and that's why I mentioned Garcia. Garcia is an Olifarian with oil investments, and we know he's a rogue.'

'We know all about that one,' said Hopeson. 'He's the one that tried to sabotage our Olympic girls' chances.'

'Yes,' said Dave. 'A year or so back he was staying in a house near West Meon. He had lost his gambling empire but then he falls on his feet again with this oil strike in Chile. By the way, one of the Olympic girls is Emily Stoneman, and she and her husband were friends of Wally Markham.'

'I've never met her,' said Hopeson. 'But I gather she was the lawyer who sent down my ex's father-in-law.'

'I know: Modlington – but I've talked to him and I'm certain he was set up by Jones and Jebbs.'

Dennis turned and looked at Cerise. 'Cerri, darling, tell him what we found out about Jones.'

Cerise had an odd expression now. 'I'm still sorry about Graham and I feel sick about the way he died, but the more I hear about his past the more angry I've become.' She paused. 'All right, this is it. My sister Jasmine has done some checking via a private investigator. You see when Graham was only seventeen he became the randy sod he always was. He got into bed with an older girl who worked at his boarding school, not another student but some sort of housekeeper. Her name was Olga Jones. She had a Polish mother and a Welsh father. She's still alive, and three days ago I met her in London. She was worried because Graham had paid her for over forty years to keep her mouth shut and she was worried she was going to lose out now he's dead. Well, I've promised her now that I'll see her all right. Anyway, she said that Graham had made her pregnant with twins. And those twins...' Cerise was tearful now and her voice breaking. 'The twins were Elwyn Jones and Amanda Jones who later married

Jebbs who killed her. Olga says both of them were twisted from the start and she could never control them. She was a young mum disowned by her parents and struggling to bring up two out of control kids. She blames herself for what happened but I've told her it can't be her fault. They inherited the genes of their father.'

Cerise smiled. 'I've remembered the name of that man on the phone. I pretty sure it was Romero. I'd never heard of him before or since.'

'We'll check him out,' said Dave. 'Do you know if he has a connection with sailing?'

'Well, I've never heard of him,' said Hopeson.

Dave said nothing but there was something in the man's tone that shouted that this was untrue. And he noticed how both of them had shied away whenever he mentioned Garcia.

Dave drove back to Alresford. He had learned things, more things in some ways than he had expected. He wondered once again how much progress the police were making. He didn't like the idea of forcing Cerise to talk to the official investigation. She had been traumatised by the original interrogation from that Marchways. Marchways was a likeable guy – the type of copper whose imagination ran in straight lines, but maybe wasn't up to a situation as complex as this. The murderers had covered their tracks skilfully so police forensic techniques probably wouldn't be a lot of help. Dave mused over what he had just learned. Why on earth should old Bigarse have been troubled about ethics when whatever was unethical was pulling in good money? It seems this enterprise was in South America and had connections with someone called, Romero. Well tracing him was a task for the Banner crime desk. Having done that Dave could report to the police himself.

He arrived at The Alresford cottage. Emily was indoors with Peter and Lily but Tom was at his firm's office in Andover.

'Hi Dave,' said Emily. 'I've got the estate agent's brochure for Lorraine's house down the road. You know – the one we were in a week ago.'

'Good, I liked it and it would suit us. You know, well placed for my work and for sailing. We'll really need somewhere like that when the baby's born.' He paused and frowned. 'What's the guide price?'

'Three hundred and twenty thousand.'

'That's one hell of a lot for a three down, one up place.'

Emily laughed. 'This is Hampshire. It's expensive, but not as bad as Dorset. Lorraine wants you to have it so she might negotiate.'

'I can't decide anything without Josie.' He paused while he sipped a welcome cup of hot coffee. 'Hey, Emily, in the world of sailing does the name Romero ring any bells?

Emily looked startled. 'Not sailing but he's the head of a solicitor's practice in Petersfield. Great guy, I worked for him for a few weeks before I joined Travis in London.'

'Well, Cerise Blake-Grass says she overheard someone called Romero warning Bigarse that he was making money through an unethical, and criminal project.'

'Why should that worry him?'

'Well, it never has before, but Cerise thought he was shocked when he was told what the deal was.'

Dave frowned and then he told her about the Blake-Grass and Jones twins.

Emily did seem especially surprised. 'Well it all begins to make sense and it seems it got Bigarse killed.'

'Emily, if you know this guy Romero could you get him to see me? We could say it's to do with house purchase and a personal problem. It's such an unusual name. I might be chasing the wrong bloke but I'd like to try.'

'No, Dave, you're supposed to have dropped out of this business under threat. Leave it to me, Romero will see me and he'll talk more freely to me.'

Chief Superintendent Hollins was angry. The Sussex murders had begun to be an obsession, but with no progress in the investigation he was under pressure to scale back on the number of officers involved. Heaven knows there was enough unsolved crime on his own patch. But he was damned if he would let this murderous conspiracy succeed unpunished. His CID subordinate, Marchway was still focussed on the Blake-Grass murder and still suspecting an involvement by Cerise Blake-Grass. Marchway was suspicious because she had apparently fallen into a new relationship with the man who had taken over running the Magnum Company. With her late husband's body still not released for burial that looked more like bad taste than a motive for murder. The investigation was now amalgamated with the same one in Sussex, and Sussex were no further forward. The journalist Manning had faded from the scene under threat. To be fair, the man had reported all the details and the New Zealand police were inclined to be helpful. But Manning was under threat himself with the attempted abduction of his wife. In one respect Hollins was pleased that this journo was no longer sticking his nose in, but on the other hand the man heard things and people told him things that they didn't tell police detectives. Also, if Manning was a target for the conspiracy, they might try to intimidate or even abduct him and in doing that they could open themselves to arrest.

CHAPTER 32

Emily was due in court in Winchester the next day. Travis had passed a brief to her for the defence of a pub landlord who had been selling whisky from bottles with fake labels, and some customers had been taken ill. The man was pleading that he'd bought the alcohol from a legitimate source and had no idea it was contaminated. This sounded dubious, but she must do the best she could with the evidence provided and leave the decision to the jury. Tomorrow she would drive over to Petersfield and talk to Paul Romero. He would probably plead client confidentiality but she might wheedle something out of him. After all, it was Romero who had given her the Smidgin brief that had made her name. Of course they were assuming a lot in thinking this was the man that Blake-Grass was overheard talking to on the phone, but Emily had checked the local telephone lists and, although Southern England was awash with Spanish and Polish surnames, there was only one Romero. This Romero's father had been a refugee from the Spanish Civil War in the nineteen-thirties who had settled in Hampshire and married an English girl. In spite of his name the solicitor could hardly have been more English.

The court was running an hour behind schedule mainly due to the freezing weather. Her client was in a surly mood and adamant about his innocence. But at the end she and he won. It was a surprise, but her cross-examination of the trading standards officer came close to reducing her victim to tears. In the end this witness admitted that they had uncovered an illegal warehouse that the police had raided not twenty four hours earlier.

It wasn't certain that this was the source of the corrupted liquor but the jury had come down in favour of the defence. Once more Emily had notched up a plus point for her career. Outside the court she retreated to the warmth of her car. There she phoned the Petersfield solicitor's office.

'Hello, young Emily. So, you won another one today,' said Paul Romero.

'How do you know that?'

'Ah, if you must know I've had a call from a colleague in court. Seems you made a big impression. How many years 'till you make QC?'

Emily laughed. 'I must have a few years to go.'

'Not that many years from all I've heard. Right, how can I help you?'

'Can I see you by appointment tomorrow?'

'Of course but what's up?'

'It's personal and involves friends of mine.'

'Emily, much as I respect you I can't disclose confidential information.' Paul Romero was firm on the point and this was no more than Emily had expected. He was a fellow professional with his own code.

'I know,' she replied. 'I thought you would say that, but we're worried. These people have abducted the sister of our friend and of course they killed Wallace Markham. He was also our friend and his wife Lorraine is distraught. And Lorraine was the midwife who delivered my little Peter.' Tough lawyer though she was Emily found her eyes moistening.

Paul had noticed and his tone softened. 'Come on Emily I'm still on your side. Let's go down to our rest lounge and have a cuppa. Then we can see if we can resolve this one.'

She pulled herself together and followed him to the lift that carried them to the ground floor of the offices. True to his word Paul rustled up a coffee pot with warm milk and a bowl of sugar. Outside in the streets the rooftops were still white with snow as passers by braved the sanded pavements. She drank the hot coffee gratefully. She could do with its warmth as she was still some distance from the ice cold car park. Paul Romero was scribbling on a notepad. He tore off and folded the slip of paper. 'Emily, I suggest you go and talk to this lady.'

'How did it go?' asked Tom.

Emily had shaken the snow off her shoes and flung her winter coat onto a chair.

'Where's Dave?'

'He drove off somewhere first thing,' said Tom. 'Did Romero help?'

'Well he was all client confidential but that means I'm on the right track and he's given me a name to talk to – and quite a name.' She passed Tom the slip of paper.

'Wow, Lady Amelia. What the hell can she know? She's a loud-voice female and she's a bloody vegetarian.'

Emily smiled. Lady Wallstead-Benham lived in the Manor House in a village a few miles away. She had been many things in a relatively short life. She had been a lawyer, like herself, before she became an MP and cabinet minister; then finally created a peer and a loud campaigner for children's rights in the third world. Her husband was a businessman and, interestingly, had connections with Dave's friend Erich Shilltinberg the Swiss computer tycoon whom she had met at Branham Lake disabled sailing. Well, she wasn't going to tell Dave that or anything else yet. It was better for both him and Josie that she handle this herself.

'Sam, can you tell me anything about Magnum?' Dave was once more in Sam Pollingham's drawing office.

Sam did not seem the least put out by Dave's direct approach. 'Yes, I've just finished working on a new forty-five foot maxi-yacht – sailing this time,' he laughed. 'You won't guess who has commissioned her.' He laughed some more. 'Well, it's no secret but he's Anton Garcia.'

Dave felt his mouth sag in shock. 'That gangster; a year ago he was broke and hiding just up the road near West Meon.'

Sam laughed some more. 'Yeah, but he still owned an oil concession in Chile. It came good with a little bit of help from his friends; or rather one friend.' His voice became conspiratorial. 'Yes, the initial money was loaned to him by Bigarse.'

Dave was not really surprised. 'They say it's a small world. I dread to think what choice words my friends Emily and Tom will use when I tell them.'

Anyway,' said Sam. 'It seems that the majority shareholding in Magnum passes to little Cerise provided she hires a reliable chief exec.'

'She's more than hired him. I met them both the other day and they seemed very cosy.'

Sam laughed. 'I've an idea she's had her eye on Denny. He's my cousin, do you know that?'

'Yes, I'm told he had a raw deal from an earlier wife.'

'My God, that evil bitch. Compulsive bloody politician – Mrs Hitler more like. Sorry about the way she died though, but Jebbs paid for that.'

'Shouldn't he have faced trial?'

'Who cares – the bastard paid for what he did. That's all I care.' The normally laid back Sam Pollingham had changed. He had a tone and an expression that Dave found unsettling. 'What d'you do to killers in your country?'

'We lock them up for a long time.'

'Don't hang'em?'

'Definitely not.'

'Well, it's not a perfect world,' Sam had relaxed again but the exchange had worried Dave. There was another side to this guy that wasn't normally on show.

Paul Romero had been as good as his word and had fixed an appointment for Emily with Lady Amelia Benham. This meant a trip to London and a visit to the House of Lords where Lady Amelia was a cross-bench peer. Emily had been to the parliament building a few times: from a school visit to accompanying Tony Travis for a meeting with MPs. This was the first time she had been in the other end of the building where the upper house met. Lady Amelia was a slightly built, almost petite woman of late middle age but with a personality that shone from every facet of her being. Emily had long admired Amelia as a feminist icon, even if Tom disapproved of her for the same reasons. They had already met her a few times at local functions in Hampshire.

'Hi, Emily – in my office. Follow me.' Amelia shot off down the ornate corridors then out of the building and across Parliament Square to a building where Amelia had her private sanctum. This was a well proportioned room and lovely and warm after the freezing cold outside. 'Right, Emily – tell all.'

Amelia had once been a lawyer herself but her sharpness and brevity surprised Emily. 'I saw Paul Romero the other day...'

'I know that. He told you about client confidentiality but I guess you know all that. Travis says you're a rising star.'

'Well, it's all to do with Graham Blake-Grass who was murdered. It seems Paul warned him that some business he was involved in was unethical.'

'Bloody hell! You can say that again. Child slave labour in South America. I'm sorry the way the man died, but he was a bastard.'

'We think it was something in his dealings that got him killed, and the man Jebbs as well. We suspect Jebbs had some blackmail hold over Blake-Grass and Blake-Grass arranged for him to be removed.' Well now she had said it. What would be Amelia's reaction?

'Emily, I can't dispute what you say. It seems more than likely and would explain a lot.'

'Was Blake-Grass a client of Paul Romero?'

'No, I am.'

'Paul won't disclose anything to me, so I didn't know who he worked for, but Blake-Grass's wife overheard a phone conversation between him and Paul. Paul told him he was making money unethically. She says her husband seemed genuinely put out when she wouldn't have expected him to care.'

Amelia smiled. It was a sadistic look rather than happy. 'Look, Bigarse – sorry that's what I called him. Well, I tried to approach him but he just yelled at me and called me a hysterical "do-gooder". So I called up Paul Romero who handles my legal matters and told him to approach Bigarse and tell him straight out that we would expose him to the media and the law.'

'Lady Amelia…'

'Hey, Emily, don't you dare call me lady. I'm not sure I've ever been ladylike. Just call me Amelia.' This time Amelia sported a toothy grin.

'Amelia, are you able to tell me what Mr Blake-Grass was doing that was so unethical?'

Amelia grinned again. 'Emily, I've heard all about your cross examination. Is that what I'm in for?'

Emily laughed now. 'No, have you ever heard of a journalist called David Manning?'

'Yes, he writes for the Banner and he had a hand in solving the Ollavasen murder. Never met him, but my husband is a Hamble yachtie,' Again the same grin. 'And I seem to remember that you were the hero of the hour as well.'

'No, that was blown up out of all proportion. I was defending my child.' Emily knew she would never forget that nightmare hour. 'Anyway, can you tell me what Mr Blake-Grass was up to and could that have been a reason for blackmail?'

'Yes, Bigarse knew a man who owned an oil concession in Chile…'

'Garcia?'

'That's it Emily and you've guessed; he's the same man that tried to wreck your Olympics.'

'Yes he did; my father's chances as well, but I don't hold any spite now. After all he destroyed his own gambling business.'

'Well, Garcia inherited this land around two hundred square miles of desert but it turns out to be an oil bonanza. The oil field is a small part of it but there was already an abandoned copper mine. Bigarse loaned Garcia the money to drill for oil but he took over the mining. That's on an area that isn't pure desert but is on the western side of the mountains and gets rainfall. Two things I found. First Bigarse and his associates were using child labour, or rather teenage kids. They were held in a camp housed and fed but not paid, so they were slaves. Then I heard in confidence that drugs were being cultivated.'

Emily had expected something like this but she was still shocked. 'Oh, God, we knew that man was ruthless but not like that.'

'Yes, but I don't know how much he knew. The operation was sub-contracted. When Paul told him the truth he says Bigarse sounded shocked but how much he already knew, Paul isn't certain.'

'I would say this was a bit more than unethical. It was criminal.'

'Oh yes, if his part in it came out he'd have been finished.'

'We think Jebbs may have found out about all this or, if not the South American crime, something just as damning. Mrs Blake-Grass seemed to think her husband was unworried by the ethics but worried about losing a profitable investment.'

Amelia replied. 'I think you know that I am a trustee of the World Child Protection Agency. There is another person who died in Sussex – a man called Jones. We suspected he was involved in child trafficking.'

'I can't see Blake-Grass involving himself in that.'

Amelia glanced at the clock. 'Sorry, Emily, I've got to get back to the House. Debate on the new rail links and I want my say.'

Emily smiled inwardly; I bet you want your say. But never mind; you've given me a nice little package of info to give Dave.

CHAPTER 33

'How's your listening out going,' Tom asked Dave.

'How would you like a Feltham Thirty-Two?'

Tom laughed. 'Well, yes if I had a spare one hundred and sixty grand in my bank.'

'Frankly that applies to us as well, but as they say it costs nothing to dream.'

'Emily's meeting with Superintendent Hollins at his own home,' said Tom. 'She learned things in London but I've told her she must keep her head down and, Dave, so should you.'

'Her London trip was good?'

'Yes, bit of a breakthrough and she'll tell you all when she's home, but we agreed she must brief the police first.'

'Hollins won't appreciate it if she's pulled a fast one on the law.'

Dave went outside into the cold with his mobile phone. He needed a good signal and it was still early evening in New Zealand. It was a delight to hear his Josie's voice and then his father's reassuring news that the two abductors had been charged and would face trial in a couple of weeks. And, better still, the police had not found any other gang members.

He was relieved, but something was continuing to worry him. All these people here in Hampshire were hiding things from him. He supposed he couldn't blame them for that. But there was something else that he couldn't connect with, an impression an intuition, a memory perhaps. Best not worry over it. Time would tell. He took out the phone again and rang the Banner offices. He was put straight through to the crime desk.

'Sorry, Dave, but Sid doesn't come in these days but here's his home number.'

Sid Everett, one time elite tabloid hack was clearly enjoying a very comfortable retirement. He opened the front door of his stylish Wimbledon detached house. ''Ello young Dave. How can I help you?'

'Hey Sid, you said this street was Cops Hill not Copse and I don't see too many trees or police.'

'Oh, you'd be surprised they were down here in force two nights ago. Looking for a Lithuanian drug syndicate in the next road.'

'Oh yeah, you hack their phone?'

Sid laughed a wheezy sound. 'Oh happier days. Can't do that no more. OK, how can I help?'

'Did you have any luck with the info I gave you on the phone last night?'

'Oh, yes, very tasty. Come on into the kitchen and I'll make some coffee. It's bloody parky out there.'

The kitchen was spacious and definitely warm. 'Gladys is out with her mates so it's gotta be me doing the honours,' Sid fumbled with a kettle. 'Anyway we know that bastard Jones was child trafficking from South America, You know – offering poor orphan kids a better life than the Rio slums. Better life? Sod that.'

'How did he get them into the country? I mean there's no free movement between there and here.'

'That's the mystery. We know the kids were taken to Portugal and somehow Jones had them shipped into the UK. Reckon he carried some drugs as well.'

'Was Blake-Grass involved?'

'What, old Bigarse – shouldn't think so. The drugs possibly, but kids – no way.'

Dave grinned. 'Sid, how do you know all this? And how long has it being going on?'

'A few years now but it's such a shame. The Banner can't run the story or a shower of two-faced politicians will want to know how we knew all this, and don't forget old Bigarse had friends in high-places – Jones too.'

Dave laughed aloud now. 'Reckon you did a bit of snide listening, eh Sid?'

'No comment,' grinned Sid.

'Have you ever met a man called Anton Primo Garcia?'

'Oh, Dave, that's an interesting name. One time Olympic sailor who tried to spike our chances in Olifa. I had a personal interest in it. I knew Steve Simpson years ago when he was under threat from a blackmailing bastard called Lindgrune; Scottish Norwegian – bad combination.'

'Oh yeah; well so was Grieg.'

'Who? What team did he play for?'

'Never mind, you know Steve's daughter, Emily?'

'Of course, Garcia tried to spike her chances in Olifa and her young man nearly got topped by a political nutter...'

'Yeah, all right, Sid, I was there as well, remember.'

'I know, but as for young Emily, I wouldn't want to be on the end of her cross-examination. Christ, if they'd had her asking the questions in that Leveson court I'd've shitted myself.'

Dave laughed again. 'I can't argue with that. But I want to know if Garcia was involved in the business we've been talking about.'

'Well, he certainly was involved with Bigarse and the oil field in Chile, but once again, he wouldn't be connected with kid trafficking.'

'What can you tell me about the mass murderer called Jebbs?'

'Right, that's the spicy bit of info I've dug up for you, but don't ask how we came by it.'

'I know; hacked from stone.'

'Jebbs was still with his wife when they all went on Bigarse's great big yacht to Rio. Bigarse got on a plane and flew to Chile and Santiago. Oh yes, here's the juicy bit. Jebbs went off to do a photo shoot in Paraguay; not porno stuff this time I gather, but his missus and Jones were free to net some vulnerable little kids. That's as far as we traced the story but my guess is they were packed aboard the Bigarse yacht and promised a fantastic luxury voyage and a new life here.'

Dave couldn't quite buy this. 'What about Blake-Grass? They couldn't hide all these kids from him.'

Sid pulled an evil looking grin. 'No, Bigarse flew home to the UK direct. That's why I mentioned Portugal. It seems the Bigarse floating palace docked there, and when it came home to Southampton the only people in it were the captain, a couple of crew, an engineer and a girl steward who we reckon was Bigarse's bit on the side.'

'Can you name these people?'

'Yeah, I've got the names here.' Sid fumbled in a cardboard folder. He read the names in alphabetical order. The crewmen and the stewardess meant nothing to Dave, but the engineer was Ternby and the captain was; well, well. Who would have guessed that one?

CHAPTER 34

The email appeared at seven o'clock that evening.

Dave, I will be on my way home tomorrow and should arrive Heathrow just after midday.
Can you fetch me?
All my love
Josie.

Dave felt an odd mixture of joy, apprehension and annoyance. The last bit he needed to suppress. A New Zealand born alpha-male would expect a wife to obey orders and stay where she had been told to stay. He knew such an attitude would not work with Josie and would put him on the receiving end of a fearsome rebuke from Emily. No, it would be lovely to have Josie home and near him and in their bed again. But they would have to be very, very careful. The things he had learned from Sid Everett had given him a sight of an even bigger criminal conspiracy than at first imagined. He had still followed his investigation but at the same time had not made it so obvious. Had he been rash? Had he given himself away to people who might not be entirely straight? The man Dennis Hopeson for a start; he knew more than he had told Dave. The man had walked into a plum job with Magnum obviously put there by Cerise. He knew that Cerise was not the one who had killed her own husband but that didn't mean that she knew nothing of the wider conspiracy.

It was Tom who broke into his thoughts. 'It's Saturday tomorrow.'

'Oh, yeah; thanks but even an ignorant Kiwi is aware of that.'

'It's weeks since we've been to Hamble to look at our boat and she's been sitting ashore in all this sub-zero weather. The roads are better now so Em and me think we'll go down to see her. Would you like to come too?'

'Josie's due in at Heathrow sometime. Could be tomorrow.'

'All right,' said Tom. 'We'll take both cars and if she phones you can shoot off up the A3 and fetch her.'

'Yes, OK, great idea and if we go to the sailing club I'll check our own little boat there.'

'We haven't got a new name for her yet,' said Tom. 'Neither Em or me think much of *White Petunia*. Em wants to cut the white bit and just be *Petunia.*'

They were standing among the packed-in sailing cruisers in the boat storage yard. 'They're going to launch her for us in early April and we'll berth her in the marina just there. It's a bit pricey but we can just about afford it even with the second kiddie arriving.'

'Huh, you can see where his priorities are,' said Emily. 'God, it's cold,' she pulled the thick hood from her fleece over her head. 'This freeze can't last forever.'

'Second ice age,' Dave laughed. 'Bit of a change from global warming.'

They walked around the little yacht. She was not the smallest in the park but at twenty-one feet she seemed tiny beside the thirty-footers. Tom's concern was the lack of work they had done in the face of the cold weather. To satisfy Emily's qualms they needed a safer bottled gas system and he hadn't yet collected their new four horsepower outboard motor. New rigging was being made along the coast near Chichester in a workshop adjacent to Steve Simpson's sail loft.

Tom was just setting up the ladder so that they could all climb aboard when it happened. Out of nowhere came an explosion, a loud thump followed by a rush of hot wind. They all turned and stared at the nearby Millennium Magnum yard. A huge motor yacht moored alongside the main pontoon was ablaze from end to end. The prevailing wind was blowing an awful stench of burning oil and fibre-glass.

'What the hell,' Tom yelled, flinched and turned away from the scene.

'That's the Blake-Grass yacht *Conqueror,*' said Dave. He took a couple of steps up the ladder for a better view then gasping dropped to the surface.

'We'd better get out fast,' Emily shrieked as she dabbed her stinging eyes with a handkerchief and pulled up the hood of her fleece. 'This air's poison.'

Tom was coughing 'Come on,' he shouted. 'Get out of here!'

The three of them scrambled for their cars and drove away. Startled onlookers were emerging from houses all staring towards the column of black smoke and tongues of flame. With Dave leading in his car they to the road bridge to the west side of the creek and stopped at the first opportunity to look back at the Magnum yard. They could see the burning yacht as a vivid red glow with the pall of black smoke wafting away in the breeze.

'What the hell caused that?' said Emily.

'About four million gone up in smoke,' said Tom. 'Tell you something though. We nearly choked because we were down wind from a breeze off the sea. You realise that means a change to warmer days.'

'But that was an explosion though,' said Dave. 'One big bang and everything goes up in the air.'

'If the Blake-Grass girl is after an insurance claim,' mused Emily. 'It's not very convincing. It looked contrived to me.'

'I'll need to go back and be a bit closer,' said Dave. 'The Banner will be interested in this and the motorboat mags, let alone the local press. It'll be big news tomorrow.'

Dave rushed for his car despite warning shouts from his friends. He sped over the bridge and round towards the boatyards. Ahead of him were a fire appliance and two police cars. The second of these turned across the road as its occupants began to reel out a police tape. Dave parked and walked towards the police, his press card in hand.

'Daily fucking Banner,' the police constable glared at him.

'I'm their yachting correspondent, so this is special,' Dave pleaded.

'Yachting correspondent! The Banner! Pull the other one.' The man glared. 'This looks like sabotage. You know anything about it?'

'We were in the boatyard back there when it happened. Then we ran because of the fumes.'

'So it wasn't you as caused the explosion?'

Dave sighed. 'I don't cause disasters. I report them. The public has a right to the news.'

'All right. Wait there and maybe we'll brief you when things calm down.' He glared again. 'You an Australian?'

Dave no longer found the question annoying. 'No, New Zealand.'

The policeman grunted and walked away. Dave could still smell the fire, an evil odour that made his eyes smart, but the choking, blinding stench following the explosion had passed. He looked around and saw a ladder leaning against a forty-foot keelboat ashore in the boatyard. He climbed the ladder and now he had a real view of the scene. *Conqueror* was burned to her waterline. There was no trace of the graceful streamlined shape that she had been. A red glow of hot ash was all that remained. Three more fire appliances had arrived and were playing pressure water onto the smouldering wreck. He couldn't see any sign of an ambulance so maybe no one was hurt or worse, burned to death. Two cars were approaching the police barrier and he knew them. It was the local TV team: Ricky Temple and his camera crew. He could see Ricky and his girl assistant arguing with the coppers. Dave didn't wait. He descended the ladder and sprinted across to them.

'Sorry, sirs,' said the policeman. 'Can't let you through yet. I understand we will be briefing you gentlemen at a special meeting this evening.'

'Gentlemen!' snapped the girl. 'Am I invisible or something?'

Dave grinned. The girl, or woman really, was thin bodied, thin faced and very tense. No, he mustn't revert to his Kiwi stereotype. He must try and be broadminded.

'I'm sure ladies will also be admitted,' said the copper. He sounded more irritated than chastened.

Dave spoke. 'Can you tell us if there's been any casualties? Do the law think this is an accident?'

'Sorry, sir. But all information will be available at the press meeting.'

The whole news team, Dave included turned away muttering. Dave pointed across to the yacht with the ladder still in place. 'Look, I was up there. There's a clear view for your cameras.'

They all climbed onto the parked yacht and the camera team muttered as they tried to stop their camera stands slipping on the icy deck. Now a diminutive figure was running down the waterside wailing. Dave looked at her; it was Cerise Blake-Grass. Dave scrambled down the ladder and ran across to her.

Cerise was clearly distraught. Embarrassingly, she flung herself at him, scrabbling with her hands before she buried her face in his chest weeping without restraint.

'Cerise, tell me, for God's sake. What's happened?'

'*Conqueror* exploded and Poppy was in her and now she must be dead.'

'All right, take it easy. Tell me what you know, slowly, and we'll see what we can do.'

Cerise released him and stepped back. She seemed to have taken a grip and the wailing had stopped although tears streamed down her face. It seemed that someone had been in that firestorm.

'Cerise, who is Poppy?'

'Oh, she's my little dog. She's the only friend I had left,' she sobbed.

Dave knew that this loss obviously meant more grief for Cerise on top of everything that had happened to her.

143

'Poppy loves being on the yacht and I left her there while I went back to my car for something. Then the bloody boat went up bang. I don't know why. It just couldn't happen.'

Dave was alert. Cerise had been aboard *Conqueror* and had turned and gone ashore.

Could she have been the target for whoever had destroyed the yacht? There wasn't much doubt in his mind that this had been a deliberately contrived destruction.

Someone pushed him aside, none too politely. It was the TV woman reporter. 'Who are you and do you know what happened to that boat?'

Cerise wailed again and collapsed onto the frozen ground. 'For God's sake,' Dave yelled. 'This lady needs to be in the warm and have medical care. Just save it until all this calms down.'

A rigid inflatable boat was cruising towards a nearby landing jetty. It was crewed by the harbour master and two assistants and one of these was holding a very wet and rather scorched terrier dog. Dave lifted Cerise to her feet and pointed. Cerise gave a shriek and raced across to meet the incoming craft. The police were still manning the entrance to the Magnum yard. Dave turned and recovered his car. There was nothing more he could do until the police held their press conference and he was not confident that they'd release anything newsworthy. In the meantime the Daily Banner would love the saga of the survivor dog. Dave's mobile phone was chiming. He pulled over and extracted the thing from his warm fleece. It was Josie.

'Darling, I've arrived at Heathrow. Should I take a taxi to our flat?'

'Christ no! Look, stay where you are. I will drive up and fetch you. There's been more trouble and I want to see you safe.'

CHAPTER 35

'The Blake-Grass woman went on that boat seconds before it blew up.' Inspector Marchway looked pleased.

'Sorry but I don't think that's going to help us. She went to collect some papers and she nearly lost her little dog in the explosion.' Superintendent Hollins was becoming annoyed with his colleague's fixation on Cerise Blake-Grass as the main suspect. They hadn't a scrap of evidence of her involvement in anything, and it seemed less and less likely that she was.

'Anyway,' he continued. 'Have forensics come up with anything? It could have been spontaneous, you know – electrical fault sparking the fuel tank.'

'The yacht's only just cooled down enough for the forensics to take a closer look. She's burned almost to the waterline and everything in her is just ashes and fragments.'

Hollins was not satisfied. This whole business was becoming a nightmare. Never had his force been involved in something so bloody obscure and insoluble.

'Tell you what,' said Marchway. 'That nosy Daily Banner reporter was in the area at the time. Funny the way he always pops up like a bad apple. And it's worse. One of my men says the Banner is claiming that old Modlington the paedo was set up and is innocent. Like hell, he had those filth CDs – caught red handed. It's that Manning that interviewed the pervert and fell for his yarn.'

'Well, it could be true you know.'

'Like hell. Sorry sir, but I can't buy that.'

'All right, Garry, I suggest you forget about Mrs Blake-Grass for the moment and wait until forensic report on the yacht.'

'Sir, what about that Manning? It's suspicious the way he's always round when these things happen.'

'No, Garry. Manning is a clever journalist but he's not a criminal. The answer is probably right in front of us; so see what you can find.'

Dave saw Josie and ran across the airport hall to greet her with a hug. She had dressed for the cold but her baby bump was evident despite her warm clothing. It was so good to see her again and he had so many questions to ask of her.

'Come, on sweetheart, let's get the car and head for home. We'll stay in the flat tonight and then go down to Hampshire in the morning. Emily and Tom insist we stay with them, but I've a date with the estate agent to discuss our new house.'

'Dave, darling. I've been worried sick about you. Those people are utterly ruthless…'

Dave smiled. 'I've been far more worried about you. I sent you to Auckland to keep you out of harm's way and then what happens.'

'Don't worry too much about me. It was poor Maggie who took the rap. Anyway she's like you, one tough cookie.'

'Did the Auckland police get anywhere?'

'Yeah, they've charged the two blokes who abducted Maggie. Seems they're pretty stupid. But the police inspector thinks they may have been involved in the murders here. That's why someone was so keen to get them out of the UK. I gather there's British police flying out to question them.'

'Do we know who that someone is?'

'Well, they both worked for Yachtiegear in this country and that's why they had permits to work in Auckland. But the fatso, Foressier used to act as major-domo at Blake-Grass's parties.'

Half an hour later they reached their Bayswater flat. Dave opened the front door and stepped inside. He walked around the tiny dwelling checking room by room. 'I hope I'm not being paranoid but I half expected some villains to have turned this place over while we were away.'

'What ever made you think that?' Josie pulled off her heavy coat and threw it over a chair.

'Dear old Sid Everett floated that idea. He thought some rival tabloid might try it, but that's not likely now. The law is getting heavy with press dirty tricks.'

Josie put her arms around his shoulders. 'I feel shattered every time we do that air trip.'

'But how do you feel, I mean the baby; is he OK?'

She laughed. 'Well, the baby is fine, but you'd better know that she is going to be a she. Your mum and dad finally made me take the scan.'

Dave kissed her. He really didn't mind one way or the other just so long as Josie was well and the baby born without harm. 'Come on, you'd better get some rest.'

'How did your court go?' asked Tom.

Emily grimaced. 'Sometimes I wonder why I'm doing this.'

'Because you're brilliant.'

'Well I won't know until tomorrow when the jury come back. Tom, for God's sake. I'm defending a lady who is a supermarket manager. She caught a couple of yobs shop-lifting drink bottles under their hoodies. She grabbed one round the neck and held him. While she yelled for security the other yob ran out of the shop. Eventually the police arrive and they release the thief and charge the shop lady with assault. The alleged victim says she tried to choke him.'

'Well, that sounds a bit off to me,' said Tom. 'What'll happen?'

'I am hopeful. The jury didn't look that impressed with the prosecution.' Emily stumped off into the sitting room and turned on the television. 'Tom,' she yelled. 'It's South Today on and they've got a report on the Magnum boat.'

Tom ran into the room. A police superintendent was speaking to camera. 'We can now confirm that the explosion was contrived and pre-meditated. An explosive incendiary charge had been placed adjacent to the full diesel fuel tank and fired remotely. This magnificent ship was destroyed within minutes, thankfully without injury or loss of life.'

'That's Superintendent Hollins,' said Emily. 'He's the one that was in charge of the Ollavasen investigation.'

'A lot of use that was,' Tom grunted. 'They hadn't a clue and it nearly lost us Peter and you could have been killed.'

She smiled. 'Well, that never happened, and anyway, it was Dave who put the police on the right track.'

'Was he at that press conference?'

'No, he and Josie are in London. Josie rang me in the lunch break today.' Emily laughed, that delightful sparkling half giggle that he knew so well. 'Josie's had a scan in New Zealand and they're going to have a little girl.' She laughed again. 'Perhaps she and Peter will grow up and have a romance.'

'That sounds a wee bit premature to me.'

Emily frowned. 'So it seems someone deliberately destroyed that yacht. Who would want to do that?'

'If they wanted to kill they didn't succeed. What about an insurance claim?'

'Unless it could be proved as malicious; no chance. If the yacht owner did it to claim insurance that would be a criminal offence.'

'I know that if I was going for an insurance fraud I'd think of something a bit more subtle than that.'

147

Emily stood up and looked out of the window. 'Hi, see who's here.'

Both of them looked as they saw Dave's Renault drive up the lane and park by the cottage. 'We really need a proper drive-in and a garage,' said Tom.

'Well, get on and do something about it,' Emily laughed.

'Not while this freeze-up goes on. You know that day the yacht blew up the wind changed south and I really thought we might be having a thaw. Now it's gone back east again. It's bloody cold out there.'

Emily went to the front door. 'Hi there, come on in you two. Josie, how are you and the baby?'

Sussex Chief Constable Fox had driven to his headquarters to find an excited CID. 'Sir,' the young girl sergeant was grinning. 'We think we've found the white van used in the Jebbs murder.'

'That sounds useful.' Why did he think of this officer as a little girl when she must be late twenties? Because he was growing old; roll on retirement in a few weeks. But first he would like to crack the Jebbs case.

In his office he was briefed with the pictures from the police helicopter. They showed a burnt out circle of scrubland with the wreck of some vehicle in the middle. Then his officers produced the site photographs. They showed a standard white van destroyed by a very hot fire.

'Where was this?' he asked.

'A mile from the crime scene,' sir. 'It's on a Forestry area but they set fire to the pine trees and that's how it was spotted.'

'More sense if they'd kept it running. We'd never have tracked it down then. I assume forensics are on the job?'

'Yes, sir, but it may be an hour or more before we even have a preliminary report.'

'Well, they never found a thing in that fake police car.'

'We know that, sir. These are clever people we're up against, but this time they may have made a slip-up.'

'We can live in hope,' Fox grunted. 'Are there any houses in those woods?'

'Yes, sir. There's an old keeper's cottage half a mile away that's been modernised and tarted up. It's deep in the woods – bit lonely.'

'Right, who lives there and did they see anything?'

'It's a holiday cottage, belongs to some business guy, but in winter it's unoccupied. But, sir, we did find tyre tracks. They're frozen in the ground just a few feet long on a grass verge and we reckon they might be the white van. There's enough front tyre left for our people to check. Sir, we've traced the owner of the cottage. He's Ifor Harris-Evans.'

'That's a name I know. Not sure from where.'

'He's a self-made millionaire. But you would know him from yachting. He owns the Yachtiegear chandlery business.'

'Of course. I buy stuff for my boat there. They seem nice people. Why does this millionaire want this holiday cottage?'

'Seems it was his marital home long ago and I suppose he has a sentimental attachment.'

'Well, if nobody was there at the time, that's not much help.'

'Yes, sir, but the team suggest we check it out because the suspects may have used it as a base.'

Fox was pleased. Maybe this would be the breakthrough. 'Well done, Sergeant. That seems a good idea.' The action was not for him to interfere. He guessed the investigation had already been doing this.

'Bloody hell, I just don't believe this.'

Jasmine Harris-Evans looked up from her book as her husband stormed into their sitting room. 'All right, Ifor. Now why don't you cool it while you count to forty and then tell all?' Jasmine was not unduly worried. These explosions of wrath were regular events but her extrovert man was never violent.

'The bloody police have issued a warrant to search our Sussex cottage.'

'What on earth for?' Jasmine was genuinely startled. *Crosshanger* was their first house when they married and she still loved it. Deep in woodland it was romantic and one of those special places where you couldn't hear the traffic on a motorway. Its isolation had charm but she had always felt that twinge of nervousness while Ifor was away on business. Even so she had regretted leaving the cottage for this superior semi-mansion.

'What for,' Ifor grunted. 'They won't tell me but I've given them a list of all the summer tenants. Can't see that any of those were into crime. It was all done through the agent and I only know one of them.'

Jasmine smiled. 'Supposing they find a huge cache of drugs. What then?'

'Oh God, girl. Don't even go there.'

'Do they want our front door key?'

'No, they've already got one from the agent.'

'Oh, Ifor, I love that cottage. I can't bear to think of it being used by criminals.'

'Good luck with the court case,' said Tom.

Emily smiled and kissed him. 'I'm not sure it's luck I need. I want sense from twelve sober jury persons.'

Tom laughed. 'Bit early in the day for them to be non-sober.'

'Well, yes, as long as they're not too hung-over we may get a sensible verdict.'

'Dave says Sid Everett was relieved that it wasn't you putting the questions in the Leveson hearing. Seems your cross examinations are becoming famous.'

This time Emily jumped with glee. 'Old Sid said that? I'm really flattered.'

'Anyway,' Tom continued. 'After work I'm taking Dave and Josie to see around Wally and Lorraine's place. I've still got the keys and they'll have a better look around without some dozy estate agent waffling away.'

CHAPTER 36

The forensic team, clad in their white overalls, were working over the interior of *Crosshanger Cottage*. It was painstaking work as they collected thin hairs from the arm chairs and searched under the furniture for anything that might give a DNA sample. It was all a bit dispiriting as they all knew that most of the occupants had been holidaymakers from the previous summer. Outside a further team, heavily wrapped against the biting cold were combing the tiny garden and the woods beyond. They had completed a fingertip search of the double garage and were now moving into the woodland. It was a female member of the team who made the find. She called out to the uniformed inspector and pointed to a hole in the earth. Her face was puckered in disgust. 'Sir, who on earth would do that? It's definitely human faeces and it looks a lot more recent than last summer.'

'Well done. Bag it up, and we'll see what the lab come up with.'

'Oh, sir, do I have to touch it?'

'Well, you've got stout gloves. I'd sooner handle shit than cut up dead bodies.'

The girl looked puzzled. 'I wonder why anyone did it out here? Look, they've fixed that pole horizontal for the person to sit on while they dump in that hole.'

'Yes, we could be in luck there. Looks as if they didn't want to leave any DNA traces on the indoor toilet.'

'Well done anyway,' said the inspector. 'It can't have been easy to spot with this snow.'

'I know but under these trees it wasn't that thick and the pole was a bit of a give away.'

'Right, they've finished indoors so next we've got to get DNA swabs from everyone who has lived in this place. The landlord is an abusive sod but we don't think he's involved. After that, it's eliminate everyone who has rented this place and that's going to take some doing as we've thirty-two names over six years and we've addresses all over the UK.' The Inspector grinned now. 'As long as the mouth swabs will do and we don't have to ask them for lumps of shit.' He began to swing his arms. 'Come on let's get out of this bloody ice hole.'

151

Emily arrived home in a much happier mood. 'Thank God, good sense prevailed. We did it; got a not guilty verdict.'

'Oh, darling, well done,' Tom put his arms around her. 'You must be building one hell of a reputation. How many have you won now?'

'Well if you include that wretched, Doyle versus Smidgin, I think I've won sixteen and lost three, but wins includes Modlington and that seems to have been a false verdict.'

'You're going places, your old boss Travis has said so from the beginning, and you heard me tell you what Everett said.'

'Yes, we've around seven months before the baby is born; then there'll be a gap before I get back in court again.'

'Well, you see that you take it easy when we get near that time.'

Emily kissed her husband. 'So, you've really come round to this at last.'

'Sweetheart, it'll make us a real family and it'll be so nice for Peter to have some competition and someone to play with.'

'Josie will have her little girl first. But how did you all get on at the house?'

Tom kissed her again. 'They're going to make an offer and see what happens. Dave's going to borrow some cash from his mum and dad. I know Lorraine wants them to have the place.'

'We'll be neighbours and that's great.'

'I worry about Dave. He's got his journalist nose on the trail. He seems determined to solve this mystery ahead of the official cops. But that could be dangerous.'

'I know,' said Emily. 'I doubt that Josie can stop him now.'

'Trouble is, the man who knew all the answers is dead himself.'

'Old Bigarse, you mean?'

'That's the one. Not much loss by any account.'

Emily gripped her husband by the arm. 'You just keep out of it. We've had enough excitement in our lives both of us.'

Tom kissed her. 'I know, childhood abduction both of us, and that prat, Garcia trying to nobble your boat.'

'Then, that psycho snatching Peter,' Emily clung to him. 'No, we keep out of this. If Dave wants to get involved then that's up to him. He's a journalist and that's what they do.'

'Well, what d'you think,' asked Dave. 'Do we make an offer?'

'The house, I love it,' said Josie. 'I feel so sad for Lorraine, but we'll make it a great family home and that's what she wants.'

'I'll call the agent first thing in the morning.'

Josie put an arm around him. 'Is anyone else in line to offer for it?'

'Not as far as I've heard. The cold weather has put people off viewing. I'd say if we want the house it's ours-in the bag.'

Dave's mobile phone rang. 'Oh, hi, Cerise, are you OK?'

Cerise Blake-Grass sounded no different in spite of her near escape from the burning yacht. 'No, David, I'm fine. Still a bit shook up but Poppy is fine now and that's all I care about.'

'Have the police told you anything yet?'

'David, that's why I need to talk to you. The police are keeping their mouths shut, won't tell me anything, but I've found something.'

'Then hadn't you better tell them.'

'Oh, no. I'm not going to get another session with that horrible inspector. He wants to blame me and send me to prison. No, David, I'll talk to you.'

Dave met Cerise in a pub that she had nominated in Petersfield. She certainly was an elegant lady and displayed no signs of the stress that she must be suffering.

'Thanks for coming, David. I need to talk.'

Dave steered Cerise to a deserted corner of the restaurant. 'How can I help?'

She leaned forwards and her voice dropped. 'My husband, Graham was being blackmailed. I did wonder why his temper was worse than ever and now I've found out why.'

'All right, Cerise, take it easy. What'll you drink?'

'Oh, just a small red wine – I'm driving.'

Dave fetched her drink and a half pint for himself. 'Now, what is it you want to tell me?'

Cerise reached into her handbag and drew out a rumpled sheet of A4 paper. She held them up and Dave could see it was covered in a string of numbers.

'That looks like wartime code,' he speculated.

She smiled. 'That's about it. You see I found all this stuff in Graham's office in our house. I was never allowed in there when he was alive, but I've had a good nose around now. Well, David, I'm not as dumb as I look...'

Dave laughed. 'I've always thought you were pretty sharp myself.'

'Thank you. Well I first found all this stuff a few weeks ago. Mike Hopeson saw it and he said he thought it was code. So last week I to it to my old uncle Jack. He's ninety-six and in a care home, but he's still mentally as alert as he was at forty. In the Second World War he was a

Bletchley code cracker. He was over the moon to see this stuff – said it was pretty basic compared with the enigma messages. Have you heard about them?'

'Of course I have. Decoding them shortened the war.'

'Well, old Jack decoded this in less than a day. He said it was a real treat as he was bored stiff in the home.' Cerise delved in her bag and brought out another smoother sheet of A4. 'The old man typed all this himself. Ninety-six and he's got a laptop.'

'Well, he must still be a high-class technician.'

'Yes, he's always kept up with the latest computer gear. See what you make of this.'

Dave to the paper and read.

0.5 million not good. Got spread 4 ways. I know what you had in the ship. 1.5 million will keep us away.

Dave looked up. 'That's pretty clear – blackmail. I've an idea what it was about as well.'

'Really,' she looked startled.

'We'll have to hand this to the police. I've got to tell them what I found out and this seems to fit with the information I was given.' Dave returned to the paper. 'Well, that's almost proof of blackmail.'

Cerise looked worried. 'I know you've got to keep the police informed, but they've got nowhere so far. And I don't want my poor uncle persecuted.'

'I doubt they'll come down hard on an old man and the fact you took this code stuff to him proves you weren't involved.'

'I don't know. That Inspector Marchway is convinced I killed Graham and set fire to the yacht.'

'He doesn't like me that much. I crossed him over the Ollavasen business.'

'I remember, that Dane – he was horrible.'

'Now, has anyone apart from you, your husband or me handled this paper?'

'No, I found them in Graham's safe.'

'Right, I'll scan a few copies and then give the original to the police. I doubt they'll find any fingerprints but they'll want to try.'

'We've had a call from that Manning,' said Inspector Marchway. 'He seems to be very thick with the Blake-Grass woman.'

'What's he got for us?' asked Hollins.

'Seems the Blake-Grass woman has found some coded message that her old man received and Manning says it's to do with a smuggling run in the posh yacht. Same one that was burned out.'

'If Mr Manning has information he will need to come in and talk to us.'

'Could those two be deliberately leading us down a wrong path?'

'That will depend on what this information is. I would guess that if Mr Manning has found something it's probably genuine. He's wasting his time as a journalist. Should have been a policeman.'

'I guess he's on a bloody sight better pay where he is.' Marchway grumbled.

Hollins smiled. 'You've never forgiven him for the Ollavasen case. In the meanwhile I've had a call from Sussex. They've found the white van, or at least there's every chance they have, and they've searched a house that they suspect was the base for the lynch mob.'

'Yes, sir, but they're only concerned with catching these murderers, but we are working on the bigger picture.'

'For which Mr Manning may be very helpful.'

It was snowing again in a steady persistent blanket that blotted out the landscape.

'Tom looked at Emily. 'You're not in court today.'

'No, thank goodness, but there's cases coming up next week and I am mandated for one of them.'

'I'm supposed to be in Bournemouth this afternoon. I only hope they keep the roads clear – or the motorway at least.'

They could hear Dave and Josie moving in the spare room. Emily smiled. 'I suppose that in this male chauvinist house you all want me to cook breakfast.'

'If you're volunteering yes, but I can do bacon and eggs.' Tom grinned at this standard early morning banter. 'Anyway, when the two kids are born and if ours is a girl, we men'll be outnumbered.'

Dave appeared looking sleepy but with a phone to his ear. 'No, don't contact anyone. I'll represent the Banner.'

Dave put the phone in the pocket of his dressing gown and looked up. 'The police are holding a press conference about the blowing up of the *Conqueror*. I'm going to be there but I doubt they'll tell us much.'

'You'd better have some breakfast first,' said Emily. 'Then we'll see about getting the cars out of here.'

Josie had appeared. She rubbed her eyes and then encircled her hands over her now distinct bump. 'Have we had any news from Auckland?' she asked.

'I'll check the computer in a minute,' Tom replied. 'Em, what are the New Zealand courts like?'

'From what I remember, a bit more laidback than ours but very thorough. I imagine the police will want to squeeze every last drop out of the kidnap investigation before the thing goes to trial.'

'I suppose if the police there find anything useful they'll pass it on the cops in this country?'

'Mutual cooperation,' said Emily. 'Any of their criminals over here will get the same treatment.'

'Won't be many of those,' said Dave. 'We're law abiding.'

'If you say so,' said Tom.

This was the second time in little more than a year that Dave had attended a police press conference in their Hampshire headquarters. As before the room was packed with journos both tabloid and broadsheet plus a few from Europe and the USA, No one was too hopeful of hearing anything sensational but then one never knew. There was a hush as the police delegation entered and sat at the long table up front. Dave noted an impressive line up with two chief constables as well as Superintendent Hollins and a senior detective from Sussex. It was Hollins who took the chair and made the opening statement.

'Gentlemen and ladies. We can confirm that the destruction of the yacht *Conqueror* was sabotage. The yacht had a full fuel tank and an explosive charge was placed adjacent to the tank and fired by remote control.' He paused. 'At present we are listing all those who had access to the yacht. We have no suspect or motive, but the late Mr Blake-Grass had many enemies.'

Hollins passed to his colleague from West Sussex. The officer reported the finding of the white van in the woodland and confirmed that it was likely to be the vehicle used in the lynching. This hedging all the way round by the police did not satisfy any of the assembled journalists. Dave wondered how many of those present knew that the yacht had once been used to smuggle disadvantaged children into the UK. The police already knew because he had told them. They had accepted his information but had not seemed particularly excited. Destroying the yacht was most likely done to destroy any forensic traces of the children. Well if the police weren't interested that left him free to follow the trail himself. The newsmen were not satisfied and the police were forced to field a barrage of questions about the lynching investigation. Most, it seemed, were less interested in the sabotaged yacht.

Dave stood up and caught Hollins' eye. 'Yes, Mr Manning?'

'My interest is in the yacht, *Conqueror*. Can you tell me anything about this explosive charge and how close to the yacht would it have been fired?'

'Yes, Mr Manning. We have studied plans of the yacht supplied by her designer and we estimate the charge to have been fired electrically from not far away.'

Dave continued. 'Mr Blake-Grasss is dead as you say. So, what reason was there to destroy his yacht and nearly kill his widow? Could that have been the motive?'

Dave detected a flicker of annoyance on Hollins' face. 'Mr Manning, your speculation is interesting but it is better left to the proper authorities.'

This led to rumbles of dissatisfaction throughout the room and after a further ten minutes of fruitless question and non-answer the police called a halt and left.

The meeting broke up to no one's satisfaction and Dave immediately called Cerise's mobile number. She answered and sounded somewhat flustered. 'Can we meet for a short discussion?' Dave asked.

'Why, has something happened?'

'I've just come from the police press conference and it was all a bit odd. I think we need to talk.'

Cerise still sounded flustered. 'Can't talk now, but ring me in an hour – OK?'

Dave replaced his mobile, found his car and drove back to Alresford.

157

CHAPTER 37

Ring in an hour Cerise had said. It was over two hours before Dave finally gave up. As a journalist he was used to people hanging up on him or fobbing him off with some lame excuse for not speaking to him. Cerise was a different case. He was certain that she trusted him and she wanted the same answers as he did. Next he tried her sister's phone; the only reply was an irritating recorded message, but it did give Jasmine Harris-Evans' mobile number. He rang that next.

Jasmine answered and she sounded puzzled. 'Have you tried the Magnum head office?'

'Yes, I did a couple of hours back. She sounded a bit worried about something and told me to ring back, but so far she hasn't picked up.'

'That's odd,' said Jasmine. 'I know she was due to go somewhere in Sussex with a client of the company. Wait a minute I'll give you her mobile number.'

Dave wrote down the number. 'Do you know who this client is and whereabouts in Sussex they were going?'

'I'm not sure, you see she rang me about the time you spoke to her and it's a bit odd...'

'Why?'

'Well, she whispered her reply about the man and Sussex. Or at least I assume it was a man but it is odd.'

Dave was puzzled. 'I would have thought a client of the boatyard would do business in their office. Do you know why it had to be in Sussex?'

'No, sorry, she didn't explain.'

'I wonder why she had to whisper into the phone?'

'I know,' Jasmine sounded tearful. 'I don't like it – that's not Cerise...' she paused. 'Look, David, I know my sister and I'm not sure she wasn't scared of something.'

Dave tried Cerise' mobile number again and only heard the usual recorded message.

Then he tried the Magnum head office. After an irritating wait he was put through to Dennis Hopeson the new manager. Hopeson, Dave had already guessed, was in some sort of relationship with Cerise and he should know where she was if anyone did. Dave explained why he needed to see her and then reported his anxiety.

'She's gone to Sussex,' said Hopeson. 'But no worries. She's in safe hands. We're thinking of moving our sales office to Chichester Harbour and we're merging it with the design office.'

Dave was still not happy. There had been something in Cerise' tone that had alarmed him. Once again he rang the Harris-Evans house. Jasmine picked up the phone and now she was also agitated.

'Dave, Cerise rang me about twenty minutes ago – something's wrong.'

'Do you know where she is?'

'Well I think so. She only spoke for a few seconds and then the phone was snatched away from her. But I know this is crazy but all she managed to say was. "I'm at Crosshanger…"'

'Where's that?'

'It's our holiday cottage in Sussex, but why should she be there?'

Dave was even more troubled now. 'Look, I've already been told that she's gone with a Magnum client to Chichester. How near is this house to there?'

'Well, it's at least twenty miles to the north. It's not far from where that horrible lynching happened.'

'Jasmine. I don't like the sound of any of this. Can you give me the address and post code of the house and I'll do some checking.'

Dave wrote down the details, and tried to make some reassuring comments. Then he went to his car and logged the given post code into the satnav. Five minutes later he was on his way. At this stage he didn't have enough information to call the police. He had an increasingly nasty feeling about this and he had to investigate and see for himself.

Cerise had always rather liked this man; until now when he had revealed himself as a brute.

'I never saw anything. I only wanted to save my little dog.' She was frightened and baffled. What could she have possibly seen in that inferno?

The man gripped her with both hands. He was strong and he hurt her. 'What did Bigarse tell you about the trans-Atlantic trip?'

'What trip?' She sobbed.

'Don't mess with me, girl. You know, that time we were all in Brazil.'

'We went out on the boat but we flew home. You know that.'

'All right then.' The brute had a hand round her throat. 'Why did you fly home? Why didn't Bigarse want the return by sea?'

She was angry now. Still rigid with fear, but her spirit was alive. 'Graham had a vital business appointment, so of course we flew home.'

'That's shit and you know it. He didn't want to be named if our mission turned sour.'

His hand was too close to her mouth and now she could sink her teeth into it. The brute swore and then banged her head against the back of the leather settee.

'Bitch, you don't leave me an option. I'm sending you where you can't talk.'

This was the final straw: fear and shortage of breath sent her into oblivion.

It to Dave over an hour to find the destination. The satnav told him he had arrived, but there was not a dwelling in sight; only leafless trees and banked up snow drifts. He parked the car in a narrow layby and began to walk. Then he saw the layby wasn't one. It was the entrance to a narrow gravelled track almost obscured by snow, but on it were the tracks of a heavy four-by-four vehicle; tracks that were recent. Then he saw the sign board covered in snow. He kicked it and the snow fell away to reveal; yes, this was it. The track was steep and Dave doubted his motor would cope with the icy slope. Reluctantly he began to walk. How he wished he had some more secure footwear than this. He needed to watch his step or risk a fall. The track wound through the trees for two hundred metres. Then, around one more bend, he saw the house with the big four-by- four parked outside. The house was a cottage, probably once the abode of a gamekeeper. Dave was puzzled. It was a freezing morning with an icy wind blast and yet the front door was open and so were two of the car doors. Something was not right and he intended to find out why.

He stepped back into the fringe of fir trees on the edge of the driveway and watched. There seemed no life and no movement within the house despite the open door and the parked car. He began to move stealthily round to the right. There lay a snow covered lawn and a bed of frozen and withered shrubs. He could see glass patio doors leading into this garden and now he could see movement. A shadowy figure was dragging an inert body across the floor. There was a single light bulb burning in this room, bright enough for him to recognise both persons. The seemingly unconscious body was Cerise and the other a burly male. Dave stiffened with real shock. He knew the man, one who, on the face of it, was the most unlikely villain that one could think of – but not so. Dave remembered now. This fellow had something in his past to hide. Blake-Grass was dead but was Cerise yet? Dave was not afraid of this man. The once top rugby player was well past his best but Dave was not. He ran across the snowy lawn and hammered on the glass doors. He could see the man and the woman clearly now. She was Cerise and the man standing over her was, the shambling untidy Sam Pollingham. Pollingham was standing over the prostrate Cerise fist clenched. Slowly he looked up and saw Dave.

Dave raised a foot and smashed the glass door open. 'Pollingham, what the hell d'you think you're doing,' he yelled.

Pollingham swung round with an angry snarl. 'David Manning, where did you come from?'

Dave surprised himself with his own calm. 'You skippered *Magnum* that time with those poor kids aboard.'

'You're a fucking journalist,' screamed Pollingham, red faced and sweaty in spite of the cold of the house. 'You're too bloody nosy for your own good. Now you're meeting your fancy girl in this house. What a shame neither of you is going anywhere.'

'Well,' said Dave. 'You are going with the police as soon as they get here.' He felt supremely calm. Here he was witness to a potential murder. He wondered what had driven this fat oaf to this point of desperation. Sam Pollingham had always seemed a cheerful laid-back naval architect: a muddled artist. Well, who could tell? Dave was a journalist and nothing about the human race any longer surprised him.

'Look, Sam, by abducting this lady, you're making things ten times worse for yourself.' He looked down at the inert body on the floor. 'Cerise, can you hear me?'

'Yes,' came the faintest of whimpers.

'What's he done to you?'

Cerise tried to sit up but sagged back again. 'He conned me here. I don't know what it's all about.' Her voice was between a sob and a whisper.

'What've you done to her, Sam? Hasn't she suffered enough these last few months? I doubt she knows a thing about your slave trading.'

'Slave trading!' Cerise's shocked tone was almost her normal voice.

'That's right. He used your late husband's yacht to smuggle in little children for sale. He took the kids in Brazil and promised them paradise...'

'Oh no!' Cerise gasped. 'It was that time wasn't it? but we didn't know. We had to fly home for Graham's business.'

'Right, that's it,' snarled Pollingham. 'You both know too much and I'm not going down to save either of you.'

'So, what are you going to do about it?'

'Do about it?' Pollingham reached behind an arm chair and drew out a shining double barrelled shotgun. 'Well, you won't argue with this beauty.'

Pollingham lifted Cerise into a chair and pressed her hands onto the gun and the trigger. Dave noticed that the man was wearing thin gloves so only Cerise's prints would be on the weapon. Then he broke open the gun and reached into his pockets for two cartridges. 'This little girl was going to top herself until you showed. What a pity you've tried to rape her. So it's one shot for you and one for her.'

Dave felt oddly distanced from what he was seeing. His common sense told him he should be scared witless but he felt calm and detached. 'Oh come on, man. Whatever you've done it's not worth murder.'

Pollingham grinned. 'I am preserving my good name.'

'Look, man, the police are on their way here. Cerise's sister has called them. She told me Cerise said something on the phone about this house. I came along ahead of them.'

Pollingham grinned again. 'If you're telling the truth then I'd better get a move on.' He pushed the gun into Cerise' hands pointed it and with her forefinger he pulled the trigger. The explosion in the close confines of the room was deafening. The recoil had sent the shots over the intended victim's shoulder. Dave felt the whine of the pellets as they passed over his head. He didn't wait; he dived at the man and hit him. The punch was meant for Pollingham's face but it hit him in the throat. The man gasped but he dropped the gun although Cerise's fingers were still enmeshed in the trigger guard.

Dave charged at Pollingnham and delivered a crunching rugby tackle that toppled them both to the carpeted floor. He continued to punch the overweight body until it collapsed.

'Trading little children as slaves. I want to kill him!' Cerise was standing unsteadily the gun in her hand and pointing it at Pollingham's head.

Dave saw enough in her expression to know she meant it. He climbed to his feet and gently to her arms and detached her from the gun. He pointed it through the open patio door and fired the second barrel.

'Hey, steady on,' called a cheerful voice from somewhere around the side of the house. 'That could be a bit dangerous.'

162

'Dennis!' screamed Cerise. She staggered through the open door onto the snow covered lawn and fell into the arms of Hopeson. Hopeson gently detached himself. 'Is Sam around?'

'In there, he's just tried to kill us.'

'But he didn't,' said Cerise. She was crying now, her body convulsed. 'David's a hero – he saved us both.'

Dave didn't know what to say. He only jerked a thumb to the door. 'In there.'

Hopeson looked inside. Pollingham was crawling painfully across the floor. Hopeson, who had been rummaging around the room, saw the security grill that Dave had failed to notice and pulled it across the door where it locked automatically.

'I expect you're wondering why I'm here,' said Hopeson.

'Well, I'm mighty pleased to see you,' Dave replied.

'Well Cerise and I have been suspicious of Sam Pollingham. Then we met Darren Ternby's girl friend; she's one Caroline Grimp. She's been to the police but they didn't seem interested in her statement. Well, Darren had told her that he'd seen Sam hanging around the Magnum dock on the night Bigarse was killed. Forty-eight hours later Darren was dead – head bashed in.'

'Ternby was ship's engineer on that trip from Brazil,' said Cerise, 'And Sam Pollingham was skipper. Nothing unusual about any of this, but supposing they had been carrying dodgy cargo.'

'Too right, they were,' said Dave. 'They'd met that man Jones in Brazil and he paid them to ship a group of street kids to the UK. They, the kids, thought they were going to a new life. Yes, they were of course but with Jones involved you can guess what sort of life.'

'Bloody hell.' Hopeson whispered.

'Graham guessed it,' said Cerise. 'I know he had a confrontation with Sam Pollignham but I never knew why. But I think Sam sweet talked him into doing something really stupid…'

'Yes,' said Dave. 'He arranged for Jebbs to be disposed of before he could stand trial and he was able to take out Jones as well.'

'But why kill that other poor man, the prison officer?'

'That's where it's personal. Wally Markham was our friend, but I suppose Pollingham and Blake-Grass wanted all witnesses to past events disposed of.'

Dave pulled out his phone. 'We'd better alert the police.'

'Already done it, there's a phone in there and I used it before I pulled that gate across.' replied Hopeson. 'But I don't like the look of the weather.'

Dave could see and feel what the man meant. Suddenly it was even colder. The sky was darker and a cold wind was blowing over the trees from the north. And now it was snowing again small flakes at first and now huge dense flurries wiping out all visibility

'Where's you car?' asked Dave.

'Down on the main road near yours.'

'If we're quick we could be out of here and away before this lot starts drifting.'

'Yeah, I thought of that but it would be better that the police came here and heard our testimony as things are. We could take Pollingham with us by force, citizen's arrest and all that, but that might weaken our story with the cops.'

'Then we'll stay here and keep the police informed. But citizen's arrest I agree with. Then we can lock the bastard up and keep him secure.'

Dave took out his mobile phone. He needed to tell Josie where he was and to reassure her. Exasperating – there was no proper signal. He stared through the patio doors but could no longer see Pollingham.

'Cerise has got the front door key,' said Hopeson. 'You and I'll go in that way and we'll find a safe place to lock our man in.'

Now Dave felt able to go to the main telephone and call Josie.

CHAPTER 38

Josie, almost ran into the sitting room. The others had never seen her look so worried.

'That was Dave on the phone. He's tried to reassure me but I'm worried. You see he's in some house with Cerise Blake-Grass and some guy and... a murderer...'

Emily stood up and hugged her friend. 'All right, Josie, slow down and tell us exactly what he said.'

Josie to a deep breath and sank into an armchair. 'He says Cerise was kidnapped by some bloke and Dave has followed them to a place in the middle of nowhere. Then, Cerise's boyfriend showed up and it's snowing and they're all stuck there and can't get out.' She began to shake and sob. 'Now the phone's cut out and I don't know what's happening.'

Emily looked up to see Tom carrying a cup of tea which he placed on the little table by Josie's chair. For once her dear husband was being tactful.

'Josie, do the police know about this?'

'Yes, there isn't a decent mobile signal but the house they're all in has a landline that was working.'

Emily gently stroked Josie's head. She was worried now. This girl was in the latter stages of pregnancy and this trauma could be disastrous. 'Josie,' she spoke softly. 'Did Dave say where this place is?'

'Yes, it's in a wood in Sussex but no one is to try and find them. He says leave it to the police.'

Tom beckoned Emily to follow him into the kitchen. 'I wonder if this place is in the same woodland as the lynching?'

'Well, we won't know that until the police have made their move. And even if we knew for certain Dave says leave it to the law and look at the weather outside.' Emily pointed through the window to where flurries of snow were already beginning to drift.

Tom walked back into the room where Josie was sitting slumped forward. He spoke gently, little more than a whisper. 'Josie, Dave said something about a murderer. Did he say who that might be?'

'Yes, but he wouldn't give a name. He just said it "will rock the boat world when everyone finds out..."'

Tom shrugged. 'That could be anyone.' He moved into the office and picked up the telephone.

'What are you doing?' Emily sounded anxious.

'I'm going to tell our Hampshire police what we've heard and I think I can even give them a name.'

'What name?'

'I've an idea, that's all. You'll only say I'm spreading rumours without court proof.'

'No, don't be silly.'

Then he told her.

At first Emily looked startled and then her expression changed. 'You could be right. There always was something a bit weird about that bloke. He always put me in mind of those two brothers who tried to kill me.'

Hopeson had found Pollingham collapsed in an armchair and seemingly slightly comatose. He recited the citizen's arrest, a British formality that Dave had vaguely heard of. They then locked the door of the room and piled a sofa against it. Outside the snow was falling faster than ever and, of course, a wind had picked up that was blowing it into drifts.

'Can't see the cops getting here all that soon,' said Dave.

'It depends on how seriously they take our call,' replied Hopeson. 'I've an idea though.' He went into the kitchen where Cerise was trying to boil a kettle on a spluttering bottle gas stove. Dave could not but admire the woman's outer calm although what she must be suffering within was anyone's guess. 'Ceri,' said Hopeson as he put an arm around her. 'I think the phone line is still working. Would you put a call through to your sister and that husband of hers and tell them what's happened and where we are.'

Cerise turned and smiled. 'Well, this is their house so they ought to know about it.'

She left the room and a minute later they heard her urgent voice. She returned and looked concerned. 'The line cut while I was talking but I've told Jasmine where we are and that there's trouble and we want the police.'

Dave felt even more gloomy. They were isolated with no communication and in the presence of a man who if given the chance could harm them all. 'Do we take turns to watch?' he asked.

'Agreed,' Hopeson replied. 'I don't trust him. I'm not sure he's really confused and concussed. And he's a dangerous bastard. He'll

166

try and make a break for it I guess.'

'OK,' said Dave. 'Two hours each until daylight.'

'And I need to put Cerise somewhere safe...'

'No!' It was Cerise and her expression was angry. 'There is only an attic and I'm not going up there, it's freezing. No, I'll stay with you boys.'

Ten minutes later the electricity failed and the house was in darkness. As the night wore on the encroaching cold began to bite. Without electric power the oil fired heating system would not generate. Outside the snowfall was blowing against the windows and drifting against the edge of the already covered lawns and garden. They were all cold. Dave pulled down some heavy curtains from the windows and they wrapped themselves in these. The coverings helped, but no one had a wink of sleep through the long hours.

Suddenly Cerise stood up. 'I've had enough of this. I'm going to light that stove and make us some tea. She walked into the kitchen and almost instantly let fly a terrified scream. Dave and Hopeson were inside the kitchen within seconds. Pollingham was there, and he had Cerise held in front of him. Just how he had managed to reach the kitchen baffled Dave for a few seconds; then he remembered and inwardly cursed. The kitchen was adjacent to the dining room and connected by a tiny serving hatch that somehow the obese Pollingham had managed to scramble through. The man must have been lurking in the kitchen listening to them.

'Look, you fuckers,' Pollingham yelled. 'Get out of this house, get walking, or I'll kill the bitch here and now.' His huge hands tightened around Cerise's throat. She struggled and gasped but could not free herself.

'Go on!' Pollingham shouted, His face had reddened and his eyes seemed to be popping from their sockets. 'Go on, get moving.'

Dave felt calm when he knew he should not be. He turned and looked at Hopeson. His companion had some sort of relationship with this poor girl. Hopeson too seemed calm although Dave could detect a tension in the man's face.

'All right, Manning,' Pollingham was literally foaming at the mouth. 'You're a useless fucking Kiwi.' He leered. 'Why don't you send for your fucking useless All Blacks.'

Despite the situation Dave grinned. Keep talking that was the secret. Pollingham was increasingly irrational or, more, likely he had the rationale of a cornered animal. 'Oh, come on, man. None of us are going anywhere. Look outside.' He pointed to the window now

167

smothered in clinging snow. 'Go on, let Cerise go. You're staying here and so are we all.' Slowly Pollingham seemed to relax and slowly unwound his hands from around Cerise's throat. The girl gasped and then staggered across the room and threw herself into Hopeson's open arms. Dave did not wait. He charged across the room caught hold of Pollingham and with a semi-rugby tackle topped the bulky man to the floor. In doing so Pollingham's head caught the edge of the fireplace fender. Blood seeped from a wound and onto the carpet.

'What do we do now?' asked Hopeson. 'Do we tie him up?'

'Better not,' Dave replied. 'We're in enough trouble as it is. He'll probably tell his legal brief that we assaulted him when he had his back turned.' Dave was worried. He knew they had shaky evidence regarding Pollignham's misdeeds and only his vicious attack on Cerise could be proved in court. 'I think we can wall him up in a room, but I don't know how bad that bump on his head is.'

Pollingham was semi-inert and groaning. Dennis Hopeson stood over him but it was Cerise who to charge. 'Let me look at that head wound,' she said. 'I used to be a nurse when I was younger.'

Hopeson looked startled. 'But Ceri, he tried to kill you.'

'Who cares,' she snapped. 'You want him in one piece when the police come.'

She knelt down beside the stricken man and examined the wound. 'I want warm water and some Dettol,' she called. 'Then look around for bandages. See if there's a first aid kit somewhere and, if not, a clean bedsheet will probably do.'

The two men looked at each other. Cerise had changed from the fragile young woman into some sort of authority figure. It was Dave rummaging around the study who found a first aid kit and took it to Cerise. She snatched it out of his hands but flashed him a quick smile. Then she set about treating the wound and bandaging the man's head. He'll probably accuse me of trying to kill him, thought Dave.

Hopeson was looking out of the window. 'I think it's stopped snowing,' he said.

Dave peered over his shoulder. Yes, it had stopped and for the first time in days a ray of sunshine was filtering through the low cloud. 'I could see if I can reach my car. It's down by the road,' he said.

Dave managed to flounder down the winding entry drive. He reached his car, now buried in a massive snow drift. That was that then; he and it were going nowhere. The road was sunken with high banks topped with leafless trees. These provided cover to the point where the road surface was visible. He remembered from his study of the ordnance map that he was only three miles from the little village of South Marshall. And it was South Marshall where Emily's parents lived. He made his decision and started walking. Clear of the trees the going was much harder. His inadequate footwear slid on the frozen crust that he was now compelled to walk on. The sunlight had disappeared and once more it was snowing, driving across the roadway from east to west while, despite his heavy clothing he was beginning to feel chilled. The snowfall was intensifying and beginning to form new drifts. He was experiencing what he knew was called a whiteout. Now he felt fear, that if he tripped and fell the snow would cover him and he might never get up again. A horrible realisation filled his thoughts as he remembered he must be within a few hundred metres of the place where poor Wally had been murdered. He resolved to stumble on. He had a duty to reach help.

Through the driving blast of snow he could just make out the telephone poles every few metres. He fixed on each one as he struggled along the way. He pulled the woollen cap further over his ears. He no longer felt cold, but the freezing air hurt his lungs. He was on an uphill gradient and that didn't help and now, thank God, he was among trees again. The snow no longer blinded him and he could see the way ahead. As he reached the top of the hill he saw a village sign post and it read South Marshall. No sign of houses as yet and he was once more stumbling amidst the driving snow. And now he could just make out a row of semi-detached cottages. He reached them pushed open a gate, staggered up the path to the front door and plied the doorknocker.

'Who is it?' the voice, female, sounded none too friendly.

'My car's stuck in a drift but I'm looking for Firs Farm. Please can you help?'

'Firs Farm, you mean the Simpson's house. That's another hundred yards on the right.'

Dave called his thanks and with relief staggered onwards. Soon he reached a driveway marked with two brick pillars. The driveway seemed interminably long, far longer than he remembered from when he drove his car up it. There in front was the remembered Georgian farm house. Ten more metres and he battered on the front door. The door swung partially open on its security chain.

'David,' gasped Kirsten, Emily's mother. 'What's happened, you look done in.'

169

CHAPTER 39

'Pollingham, I can't say I'm all that surprised,' said Steve Simpson. 'I like to think I'm a judge of character and that guy may be a good laugh but there was something about him – you know a sort of manic...'

Steve and Kristen had almost pulled Dave into their house. Kirsten had allowed no explanations until he had been put in a hot bath, fitted out with dry clothes and fed two sugared cups of coffee. Then he had blurted out the whole story.

'I know that cottage, said Steve. 'Is the phone still dead?'

'It was half an hour ago,' replied Kirsten. 'I tried to ring Emily, but no luck.'

'What about a mobile signal? I think it's time to report this straight to the top.'

Kirsten glanced out of the window. The snow had eased a little but was still falling. 'I'll get a signal a little way up the hill.'

Steve looked concerned. 'You will be careful. It's very cold out there.'

Kirsten laughed. 'Cold, I am a Scandinavian. We used to walk the Norwegian mountains in winter – so no problem.'

'David,' said Steve, 'Do you know the name of this cottage you were on about?

'Yes, it's Crosshanger; sounds pretentious as it's only a small place.'

'Good, Kirsten you'd better ring Fox direct. He'll listen to you. And then ring Emily and tell her what's happened. She can tell David's wife and put her mind at rest.'

Kirsten donned her coat, boots and hat and they watched as she strode across the whitened garden through the gate and up onto the hill.

Steve stared at Dave. 'Surely you're not telling me that Pollingham was behind the lynching of Jebbs?'

'Oh no, Blake-Grass orchestrated that with hired hit men. We may never prove it as the man is dead now as well. But I think we can prove that Pollingham killed B-G and then he killed Ternby the only witness who saw him at the scene.'

'But why?'

170

Dave told him about the hi-jacked Brazilian children.

'Oh God, that's vile. Are you telling me that Blake-Grass was involved?'

'No, I doubt it. He had flown home but it was Pollingham who skippered the yacht with the kids aboard. No doubt the crooks behind it paid him well.'

'How on earth did he think he could smuggle them past immigration?'

'They left them in Lisbon and then sailed home. Maybe the market for them was in Portugal; after all that was the children's native language. My guess is that Jebbs planned the crime with Pollingham and when B-G found out he had both Jones and Jebbs killed. He didn't dispose of Pollingham. I guess he thought that would be a step too far. Pollingham was only the boat's skipper and he could still be useful. Bad mistake by B-G because it got him murdered as well. My guess is that the engineer saw something from the dockside and that meant Pollingham had to dispose of him as well.'

Steve grimaced. 'I've had a lifetime in the boat business but after this and the Ollavasen killing, let alone what happened to our poor Emily when she was a kid, then that idiot Garcia in Olifa. I'm not sure it isn't time for me to back off and retire.'

'Your family do seem to be unlucky.'

'I suppose so, but I've always thought sailing was about happy relaxation, but in my lifetime I've seen it attract skulduggery on an epic scale. It's put my family in danger let alone the Olympic medal fiasco. Emily's Tom was lucky to come out of that alive.'

Kirsten staggered back indoors again. 'I've spoken to Norman Fox,' she said. 'My God it's cold out there, as cold as Norway ever was.'

'What did he say?' asked Steve.

'Well, he asked a lot of questions but I told him I only knew what David here had told us. Then he groaned a bit but then said he would take this seriously but he couldn't see how they could reach this Crosshanger House today now all the roads are blocked again.'

Dave looked worried. 'I think they ought to try. That guy is crazy and he's like a cornered animal. He's already tried to kill little Cerise.'

'All right, David,' Kirsten was grinning now. 'He told me that they couldn't go by normal means but he accepted this was an emergency.'

Dave sighed. 'Let's pray they don't find blood and disaster when they do get there.'

'I've locked him in the bathroom,' said Dennis. 'And I think he's played into our hands this time.'

'You really think so,' Cerise looked doubtful.

'Oh yes, he's seen a bottle of whisky in the kitchen. Made a grab for it but I stopped that. Then I thought about it. So I took the bottle, it's less than half full anyway and I dropped a few sweeteners in it.'

'How come?'

'In the kitchen there's a medicine cabinet and a nice little bottle of Tamazapan tablets. So I tipped them in with the scotch, or not all of them, we're not going to kill him, but just enough to lay him out for twelve hours.'

'With all that alcohol, probably longer than that.'

'So, Cerise, darling. You are safe.'

She looked pensive. 'I only hope Dave has reached the outside world. It's so cold...'

They prepared for another cold long night. Hopeson checked and confirmed that Pollingham was lying on the bathroom floor, comatose and snoring.

It was a little after dawn the next morning. The snow reflected the early light and the sky was still lit with stars. To the east there came a musical bussing with a bright light in the sky. Three minutes later they saw the police helicopter. It zoomed low over the house, circled and gently subsided on the wide front lawn. The rotors blasted a whirlwind of snow across and over the house windows. Cerise squeaked in alarm as four black clothed figures jumped to the ground and sped towards the house.

'It's all right Ceri,' said Mike. 'It's the cops. Well done Dave, he must have made it to somewhere.'

CHAPTER 40

Emily ran down the beach waving a sheet of paper. 'Tony Travis has just emailed me.'

'How is it going?' asked Tom.

'Well, it was a bit sticky at first. Pollingham kept his mouth shut in the police interrogation – wouldn't admit anything. But Tony's had a bit of a breakthrough.' Emily subsided breathless on blanket covering the patch of beach where her friends were sunning themselves with the heavily pregnant Josie swathed in a light wrap.

'Have they got the kid from Portugal?' asked Dave.

'Yeah, he's allowed to give his evidence on a TV link with an interpreter but he put on a good show – very convincing. But then Tony's been given some photos of *Conqueror* docking in Lisbon and they show Pollingham supervising the unloading of the kids.

'But can they prove evil intent?' asked Tom.

'Yes, that's it. In this case the Portuguese police have been co-operative. They found the kids are working as slave labour in rich houses and farms although there doesn't seem to have been any sexual molesting.'

The four friends were relaxing on a sandy beach outside Auckland on a warm early March afternoon. England and Hampshire, the freezing winter and all their troubles were a world away.

'But he's got to prove the murders,' said Tom.

Dave opened his eyes. 'The police did drop it to me that they've taken dozens of DNA samples from the Ternby flat and the poor man's girl has given them something sensational.'

'I know,' said Emily. 'The girl said Ternby had told her he saw Pollingham on the dockside not long before B-G was clobbered. But there's no corroboration. It's up to the jury to believe her.'

'Dave,' asked Emily. 'Did you suspect Pollingham?'

'Well. I always thought there was something odd and manic about the man. Then there was that email that Cerise found: listed a whole lot of people including somebody called Iver. Well, we all suspected Ifor Harris-Evans, but he spells his name with an f and an o. But I knew there was a character we called "I've a". You know he was always saying "I've an idea" and "I've a good feeling about this". That was Pollingham. He was so persistent that some people called him "I'ver", or "I've a fiver" though I doubt he ever said that.'

Tom grinned. 'It did occur to me too, but I thought it far fetched.'

Dave glanced at Emily. 'Has your Dad been called yet?'

'Tony is hoping he won't need to. Dad only heard Cerise make a cryptic remark at a party. But he's calling her anyway and she can explain.'

It was the bravery of Cerise Blake-Grass that had most impressed Dave. Pollingham was setting up to kill her before they had intervened. Did he really mean to commit one further murder? Dennis Hopeson was Pollingham's distant cousin although the two had had little contact over the years. Now it was clear that Cerise was in a serious relationship with Dennis who would no doubt be a more relaxed partner than old Bigarse. It was almost certain that the two thugs now in custody not a mile away were involved in the Jebbs lynching. The New Zealand police were expecting long sentences for the snatching of his sister Maggie. He doubted that any extradition order from the UK would cut much ice when two Poms had committed a local crime that had the whole two islands of New Zealand buzzing.

'Come on, 'Emily called. 'Who's coming in for a swim.' Suddenly she was no longer the rising young barrister or the expectant mother. With a joyful yell she ran down the sand and into the warm sea. The others followed and for a happy half an hour they all splashed and laughed as if they were children again.

Next day Emily received another call. She went into their rented holiday home and found the others. 'Tony says we've won half the battle. Guilty for the two murders. Guilty for helping to trade the children, but not guilty for sabotage of the yacht. And not guilty for the murder of Jebbs and Wally.'

'But that was Bigarse's work wasn't it?' said Tom.

'That's speculation but as all the parties involved are dead we may never know.'

Dave intervened. 'The prosecutors here say they may be given permission to include those killings in the charges of the two thugs they're holding.'

Emily looked doubtful. 'Can they do that for a crime in a foreign jurisdiction?'

'That's where it becomes political, but I think there's a chance.'

'If they killed poor Wally,' said Emily, 'they need to go down for a long sentence.'

'We're a bit more liberal than the UK but I guess they wouldn't see the light of day for thirty years. Likely they'll serve most in a UK jail.' Tom looked gloomy. 'It's fantastic weather here but we're booked on a flight home next week and I've got to be back at work.'

Dave laughed. 'World weather reports that Southern England has had an amazing thaw with floods and mayhem all round. Anyway I'm not going there just yet. The Banner wants me to report on the squad training of the All Blacks. They're coming to annihilate the Poms.'

'Don't bank on it,' said Tom. 'Em, has Pollingham been sentenced yet?'

'Yes, Tony phoned me an hour ago. Minimum twenty five years.'

'One good thing,' she said. 'Old Ferdy Modlington has been exonerated. His appeal succeeded and he's completely cleared. He's going to law against the tabloids for libel.'

'That's not good for your reputation.' Tom sounded worried.

'Don't care. Even though I won that case I was never happy with it.'

'Don't worry,' said Dave. 'You'll win plenty more. The Banner's crime reporter told me so.'

Now she laughed. 'I'm not sure that's much of a recommendation.'

'Oh God,' said Tom. 'When are we going to be allowed a normal life?'

Josie spoke. 'I'll never forget that awful day when we saw Peter abducted.'

Tom put his arm around his wife. 'Em, you saved our Peter. You're an amazing girl.'

Emily turned and kissed him on his cheek. She glanced at their friends. 'Do you know that when we were children both Tom and I were kidnapped by different mad people?

'I know about your misfortune,' said Dave. 'But what happened to Tom?'

'He was grabbed by a mad Australian woman who tried to throw him over a cliff.'

'Aussie woman...' Dave shook his head and grunted.

'When we were in Olifa another crazy woman tried to kill Tom.'

'I know,' said Dave. 'I was in Olifa at the time.'

'No,' said Tom. 'From now onwards we are all going to live normal untroubled family lives.'

Emily laughed. 'How very boring.'

THE END

By the same author

THE NEMESIS FILE

Professional yachtsman and Olympic medallist Steve Simpson has problems. His wife has died and his Chichester sail making business is under threat. When Steve and his daughter Sarah find the body of a young Dane in the sea off the Sussex coast they are inextricably sucked into an international blackmail and drugs conspiracy.

The story describes fourteen days in the late summer of 1990 that will change Steve's life. It is a test that leads him to new love and a rebirth of his hopes.

This tense mystery-thriller moves swiftly from Sussex to Copenhagen with interludes in Portsmouth, Italy and Scotland, and ends with a sea chase in a gale

ISBN 978-0-9548880-0-8 (0-9548880-0-6)

Available from Benhams Books
1 Fir Cottage, Greatham, Liss, Hampshire GU33 6BB

Reviews of *The Nemesis File*:

Journalist Pamela Payne: With locations as diverse as the South Coast of England, Naples and Denmark, *The Nemesis File*'s credible sailing scenes will either have you reaching for the seasickness-pills or signing on for a course; the sex scenes, however, are the most romantic I have read for along time. A great adventure story, which will delight both sexes – sailors or landlubbers."

Yachts and Yachting December 2004. "...Jim Morley is a sailor writing for sailors and his first novel is immersed in the South Coast yachting and dinghy scene...if somebody was going to write a novel for *Yachts and Yachting,* readers this would probably be it.

Yachting Monthly: 2006. Dell Quay based yachtsman Jim Morley has turned his hand to writing thrillers based on his sailing experiences of forty years. His first novel, *The Nemesis File,* is a murder mystery linking a Chichester sailmaker with a failing business, the corpse of a Dane found floating off Sussex and Nazi propaganda minister Josef Goebbels.

Reviews of *The Nemesis File* (continued):

Olympic sailor and coach: Cathy Foster, 11th Dec 2004

Rarely have I read such a racy book! It's carries you along at pace, and holds you fast until the very end. Just then, you think that maybe this is getting far-fetched, but the punch-line pulls you up short, and makes you re-assess the characters and their relationship to events. Suddenly the plot hangs together again in a very satisfactory way, just as good detective stories should.

Instead of long descriptions to 'paint a picture' of all the venues and situations, the writing is succinct and carefully crafted to give the maximum impression for the minimum words. This gives the book its fast tempo, yet nothing is lost because the accurate detailing of locations and action bonds the reader into plot. As a past Olympic sailor myself, I know the sailing venues described in both Chichester Harbour and Copenhagen well, and I can reassure any future reader that the author has definitely done his research. In addition, he's right – you do build life-long bonds with other British athletes and other countries' sailors when you are part of the Olympic team representing your country. It is a pleasure and highly unusual to read a book which describes the joys of sailing and racing so well. Yet it's not a book about sailing, full of technicalities of the sport. Sailing provides the background framework for a story of murder and blackmail where the investigation chases over four countries and three generations of lives. A thoroughly enjoyable read.

Cathy Foster went to the Olympics in 1984 (finished 7th and made history as the first woman helm since the 2nd World War) and competed in two other Olympic campaigns, the last being 2002/3. She's a freelance Coach who specialises in top level racing, including Olympic and Paralympic sailors

By the same author

ROCASTLE'S VENGEANCE

When out of work sea captain Peter Wilson takes a job as harbour master in the Dorset yacht harbour of Old Duddlestone, he is surprised to learn that his own father, James Wilson, was the harbour's wartime commander.

There are unsolved crimes involving this secretive community dating back fifty years. The deaths of the entire personnel of a research laboratory, then a rape and murder followed by a lynching.

Peter, aged ten, witnessed his father's suicide. Now he hears disquieting rumours about his father's dubious activities in Duddlestone. He forms a relationship with single-mother, Carol Stoneman. When Carol's ten-year-old son is abducted, Peter is forced into a situation that nearly bring his own destruction.

This mystery thriller is set on the Dorset coast in the summer of 1997, with a sailing background.

ISBN 978-0-9548880-1-5 (0-9548880-1-4)

Available from Benhams Books
1 Fir Cottage, Greatham, Liss, Hampshire GU33 6BB

Reviews of *Rocastle's Vengeance*:

Unsolicited comment on Amazon. *****
Wow! What a read. You know it is a good book when after a few pages you don't want to put it down, nor answer the phone, door or anything...

Bournemouth Echo, July 2006.
Novelist brings mystery to the coast.
Rocastle's Vengeance, James Morley's second novel, is brimming with references to Purbeck Poole and Bournemouth. The book recounts the tale of a harbour master who uncovers murky secrets when he takes a job in the imaginary village of Old Duddlestone...

Tim O'Kelly. Whitbread Prize judge southern region.
Jim Morley writes with skill and intelligence: a genuine storyteller in the finest tradition.

By the same author

MAGDALENA'S REDEMPTION

If an eight-year-old boy commits murder is he irredeemably evil? Can he ever be rehabilitated or will he kill again to preserve his secret? Hampshire farmer, Tom O'Malley, finds the dead body of a young journalist. Not satisfied that she is a suicide he makes his own investigation.

Fed rumours about his friend and employer, Hollywood film director Gustav Fjortoft, he angrily rejects them. Yet all his inquiries into his friend's past seem to substantiate the rumours.

Following suspicious deaths in his own community, Tom's quest leads him the American West Coast, where he escapes abduction and near death.

Returning to England he finds the answers he seeks in a dramatic finale in his home village.

ISBN 978-0-9548880-2-2

EMILY'S HOUR

Everything changes for the Simpson family when the dead body of an internet millionaire is found in Branham Lake and a close friend is falsely accused of murder.

It is 2004 and Steve and Kirsten, the central characters in James Morley's first novel, The Nemesis File are now married and have settled in rural Sussex with their children Emily 13 and John-Kaj 8. Steve runs the family nautical business near Chichester but teaches sailing at Branham Lake on the Surrey Hampshire border.

When further deaths occur, a police inspector facing a mental breakdown is convinced of his suspect's guilt. While Steve and Kirsten fight to clear their friend's name they have no inkling of the nightmare that is to engulf them. When Emily, along with an elderly war veteran, is abducted by a sacrificial religious cult, the family become the centre of worldwide attention.

Emily's Hour is a tense thriller, with a background in sailing that will engage both adults and teenagers alike

ISBN 978-0-9548880-3-9

Available from Benhams Books
1 Fir Cottage, Greatham, Liss, Hampshire GU33 6BB

By the same author

OLYMPIC NEMESIS

Emily Simpson's Olympic dream is threatened by an internet gambling syndicate.

Emily and crewmates Chloë and Erin are selected to sail for Britain in games held in the mysterious South American country of Olifa. Emily's father, Steve, is sailing in the Paralympics. Speculation about a father/daughter double gold puts both under threat.

Former Olympian Steve recovers from a stroke to rediscover his love of sailing.

Emily's Danish mother, Kirsten, lives in the shadow of her family's wartime disgrace. Rumours circulating about Emily's ancestry bring her and partner, Tom, into danger from a deluded stalker.

ISBN 978-0-9548880-4-6

FLANAGAN'S LEGACY

An international conspiracy in 1919. The killing of children in a Spanish village in 1937. Distant events come back to haunt the lives of Clare O'Dwyer and Michael Walters a young couple unborn at the time of either.

It is the early summer of 1994. Clare has inherited the fortune of her grandfather: US Senator James O'Dwyer, war hero, rogue politician and last survivor of the Flanagan Plot. Even after seventy years the truth would cause a fatal breach in relations between the United States and Britain.

Clare has no knowledge of this plot but is not believed. She is threatened by both security services and terrorists. To escape the pair run away to sea in their sailing yacht *Quadra*. The voyage takes them from France, Dorset, Cornwall and finally West Cork. They are abducted by terrorists and survive a force ten gale off Southern Ireland. In a dramatic climax Michael narrowly escapes with his life and Clare discovers something about her grandfather that will change her life for ever.

ISBN 978-0-9548880-5-3

Available from Benhams Books
1 Fir Cottage, Greatham, Liss, Hampshire GU33 6BB

By the same author

TANGLED RETRIBUTION

Did a half-million dollar bribe to throw a yacht race lead to the brutal murder of a yachtmaster? Why should this threaten Emily Stoneman and her newborn baby? When further murders occur it seems a psychopath is loose. Yacht journalist David Manning makes his own investigations with startling results.

Tangled Retribution is a tense detective novel involving characters from James Morley's previous sailing thrillers.

ISBN 978-0-9548880-6-0

SONG OF SUSSEX

Song of Sussex is a new departure for James Morley. A historical saga covering most of the last century and some of this.

The story is the fictional life of Richard Dyer, a boy born on a Sussex farm in 1920. Richard has a gift for music that takes him from humble birth to world-wide fame. The story has something for everyone: music, 1930s London, flying with the RAF in World War 2, then the post-war world where Richard achieves his triumph.

Richard has a tangled love life that causes his Australian wife, Stella to drag him back to her homeland. The story ends with Richard the farm boy honoured in every country and continent. The city of Chichester and the county of Sussex resonate through the story. And there is plenty of sailing.

ISBN 978-0-9548880-7-7

Available from Benhams Books
1 Fir Cottage, Greatham, Liss, Hampshire GU33 6BB

By the same author

LIFE AND LOVES IN SHINKLEY

Bluntly spoken Yorkshire man Simon Robsby leaves the army for a job selling farm equipment in Sussex.

He and his wife Angela (Angie) and two children Lizzie and Mark settle in the pretty village of Shinkley notorious for its strange cults.

But Simon has a dark secret that Angie must never know.

While exploring the woodlands his children rescue an abused runaway child and take her home. The family adopt little Anna, settle down to life in their new home and make friends.

But can Simon keep his dark secret from Angie?

Life and Loves in Shinkley is filled with pathos, humour and affection for the Sussex countryside and its people.

ISBN 978-0-9548880-8-4

Available from Benhams Books
1 Fir Cottage, Greatham, Liss, Hampshire GU33 6BB

www.ingramcontent.com/pod-product-compliance
Lightning Source LLC
Chambersburg PA
CBHW072143170626
46813CB00004BA/1653